The following was committed to print with painstaking accuracy. Every attempt has been made to portray the particulars in a fair and objective light.

While the structures and citizens of Venice Beach are true to life, the locations of certain establishments, and the identities of several persons, have been altered for the sake of the community, and for the privacy of those individuals whose lives were so brutally disrupted.

This said, the author cannot guarantee that events drawn from memory are one hundred percent accurate, for, as this account will amply reveal, eyewitness memory is never one hundred percent reliable.

Freak

Also by this author:

Microcosmia

Carnival

Signature

The Deep End

Legerdemainia

ronsandersatwork.com

Freak

Chapter One

Purly

The vanity mirror's dozen rose bulbs flickered every time a neighbor switched on a major appliance. This flickering, barely perceptible under hard white light, was a dramatic event in Marilyn Purly's perfectly dark bedroom.

Her ceiling and walls were papered black, her furniture ebony-stained. Carpet, bedspread, pillowcase and sheets: all were dyed *Midnight*, the deepest black available. Floor-length black velvet curtains hung in her windows and doorway.

But for Purly, the little black room could never be dark enough. That reflection belonged to a golden touch-me-not goddess; on the inside sick and dying, on the surface uniquely and breathtakingly attractive. Purly's uniqueness, in heavily cosmeticized Southern California, came partly from being damaged goods, and partly from being an unadorned natural beauty surrounded by gaggles of underdressed posers. Through no fault of her own, this *wounded nymph* quality came off as a direct challenge to men, and as a slap in the face to women.

In one of nature's crueler little ironies, Marilyn Jayne Purly had been cursed with a pathological aversion to attention. She'd tried hoods and bonnets, scarves and veils, bangs and dark glasses; nothing could conceal her sexual charisma. Even the suffocating wraps she wore outdoors seemed only to cling and entice. Though countless young women would have killed for her looks, Purly's deepening depression inevitably drove her to the opposite idea. It took eleven suicide attempts and half a dozen complete nervous breakdowns, but in the end the most aggressive men withered and ran. Her fiercely protective land-lady took care of the rest.

The hospitals and courts agreed: whether institutional-ized or subsidized in the real world, Purly would not survive outside her bubble. Only a steady stream of S.S.I. checks kept her safely sealed in this crypt.

All her life she'd dreamt *plain*; Marilyn's make-believe self was a wisp of a woman, daintily dancing for gentlemen in denim. One, the nicest one, would sweep her off her feet to a land of coffee mugs and white picket fences. The mirror was her window into this secret world. Purly began reliving her tortured adolescence in that little window; initially as a distract-ion, then in direct competition with the fantasy. In time the deli-cate dream dissolved completely, leaving her addicted to a masochistic morning ritual.

Looking into that swirling glass pool was like watching a movie on a flat oval screen. She could see the halls, could hear the whistles and shouts, could almost smell the hormones as the boys of high school came stampeding; hurling themselves a-gainst her, squeezing frantically, blocking her progress as she struggled to make class. Right behind were the average girls, egging the bug-eyed boys on, slapping her too-pretty face until she ran the gauntlet screaming like a banshee. Alone in the dark, Purly still felt the boys' horny paws, still felt the normal girls beating her into hysterics.

Closing her eyes, she reached into her makeup box, picked out an unused razor blade, and guided it to her face. The jerking blade never touched flesh, but she felt every imaginary slice before lowering it to poise, for the thousandth time, above an upturned wrist.

Purly opened her eyes, neatly returned the blade, and for the thousandth time watched the ghosts of adolescence drift to the mirror's periphery.

Fresher, sharper images rose in their place. First up was her landlady's toad-like face, her fat eyes burning through the shadow of a straw hat's brim. Next appeared the probing face of a serious man, a kind of senior policeman. Lastly came the crouching form of a muscular man facing away, the back of his jumpsuit lettered, enigmatically, HARBOR TV & VCR. These images also drifted and passed. The mirror clouded.

Out of the fog rose an angular face with gray, very penetrating eyes. The eyes had a way of locking onto your movements without shifting, as on one of those imposing portraits with eyes that appear to pursue you regardless of where you stand. Immediately behind the face came a dully resonating sound, like a buoy's bell in choppy waters. The sound produced a conditioned response: Purly placed a hand in her makeup box and extracted a tiny vial of perfume. She twisted off the cap. The ringing grew insistent. She let a few drops fall into her cleavage before loosening the big satin bow on her sweet little babydoll.

Now the doorbell was clanging urgently in her skull. In a dream, she pushed herself to her feet, pulled aside the curtain, and staggered around the jamb. The bell had her by the pulse. She almost fainted when she reached the door.

Daylight was a vertical splash of acid. Purly clung to the knob while the man outside cursed her up and down; first with gentle urgency, then with real invective. Once she'd freed the chain he forced the door with a foot and forearm, steadily bumping her back until he could squeeze inside. Juggling a sloppily stuffed black plastic bag, he slammed the door, shoved the chain back in its catch, and firmly turned the knob's heavy new, deadbolt-style lock. Vilenov dropped the bag on a coffee table and peeked between the curtain and window frame. Yes, there she was, right on cue. That fat nosy witch with the humongous straw hat, sneaking out of her apartment to pace the drive. He let the curtain fall.

An edgy, lean little man, Vilenov moved in fluid spurts. In another unbroken sweep, he switched on the ceiling light with his left hand, scooped Purly by the waist in his right arm, and eased her onto the couch under the high wide mirror in the chipped plaster frame. He plopped down beside her excitedly, ripping open the knotted bag with his teeth. Inside were a fifth of Jack Daniels, a few hundred dollars in tens and twenties, and a number of hardcore pornographic magazines. He spun off the cap and swallowed greedily before tearing away a handful of cellophane. "Gifts," he mumbled, his eyes gleaming. "I come bearing gifts." For a while there was nothing to be heard but the rustle of thumbed pages and an occasional swallow. At last he sighed and fell against her, a forearm balanced on her shoulder. The hand dangled only a moment. As it began its slow descent he dropped back his head.

"Oh, Marilyn, Marilyn, Marilyn; oh sweet, sweet *sweet* Mary Jayne. How I've missed you, sugar pie. And you never even knew I was gone, did you?" He eased down the babydoll. "But I told you I'd be back. Just like always."

Purly stared ahead without expression. Hugging her in his left arm, Vilenov bent forward to peel off his shoes and socks. *"Mary Jayne!"* he hissed, pulling her back with him. "It's on fire in here, don't you think?" It was like talking to a rubber doll. "But that's August for you. Even the ocean air doesn't help much." He lifted her hand and placed it on his thigh. The hand was cold as putty. "Why, I remember walking barefoot on the beach as a kid, and the sand would be so hot I'd come home with blisters on my feet. That kind of heat—August heat—gets sucked into anything that's holding still." Vilenov rocked against her playfully. "But enough about me. I know you must be sick of hearing about my crummy childhood." He peeled off his shirt, spat out, *"Damn,* it's hot!" and grabbed a handful of golden hair. Vilenov yanked her head around, his bitter gray eyes narrowing. "You've never *told* me, sweetheart. Just what are you hiding from, anyway? You think you're too good-looking for the rest of us? Is that it? You think we common folk will just catch fire and explode if we have to endure even one *teensy* peek at your precious, intoxicating beauty?" He shoved her head so hard the cartilage in her neck popped. Purly's chin rolled shoulder to shoulder, at last coming to rest buried in her chest. Vilenov ran his tongue through her long damp hair, grimacing at its sweetness. "Honey Blonde," he mumbled. He pulled her head back up, but this time with tenderness. "Listen, *lover*, before I started doing you I had 'em all, and like any sane male I went for the youngest and prettiest, the dumbest and blondest tail I could find—models, beach bunnies, playgirls; you name it. Not so very PC you think? Not *sen*sitive enough? But that's how we men are. We're hardwired for action, not for airs." He turned her drooping head to face him and spoke like a confident suitor about to pop the question. "Well now, Mary Jayne, let me tell you. For twenty years I've been peeling back the primest poon this county has to offer. But you know what? Sooner or later a man grows up. Sooner or later he realizes that all those snotty plastic bimbos out there are purely superficial, and finds himself going after...strange fruit." He released her head and shifted tighter against her, whispering in her ear while his hands roamed. "You don't know what I'm talking about, do you? You don't know who I am, or how many nights we've spent together, or just how crazy I am about you. Or how happy it makes us both when your pretty little nightie comes sliding down...it's so pretty...*so* pretty." Vilenov shuddered as Purly's babydoll dropped to her waist. He moaned, pressed down her hand and slid it up his thigh.

The hand resisted.

Vilenov froze, every sense questing. For half a minute he didn't even breathe. Then, very slowly, he reached over, gently pinched her chin in his fingers and turned her head. Purly responded with a petite cough, flecks of froth emerging at the corners of her mouth. In Vilenov's pale gray eyes a pair of red blazes appeared and passed. He carefully studied the slack, heartbreakingly lovely face. "That chest cold of yours is getting worse, Mary. We'll have to do something about it. Now you just sit here like a good girl while I go get the medicine. Don't make a move." Vilenov rose and stood absolutely still, feeling the room. He listened closely, studied every object visually, sniffed the air for unfamiliar scents. Sweat was building round his hairline, rolling down his chest and back. The place was a freaking sauna. He took another long look around and tiptoed into the bathroom.

Purly sat in a slump, staring at nothing. She thought she could hear voices outside, very much subdued. Whispers. There were also a few miscellaneous sounds: the soft turning of gravel underfoot, what might have been a radio chattering in the distance, a familiar creaking of floorboards in the apartment above. Then, except for the tiny squeaking of the medicine cabinet's hinges, complete silence. Without knowing why, Marilyn Purly wobbled to her feet. She walked to the front door in a trance, noiselessly unlocked the knob, and returned to her place on the couch. Her eyes fell on the black oblong box of the VCR, squatting atop her television's dull maple cabinet. *Hello*, she wanted to say.

Vilenov walked back in; a jar of Mentholatum in his left hand, his trousers and briefs in his right. He tossed the clothes on the coffee table, liberally lathered his hands with the mentholated goop, and turned to face the hunched woman. Their knees locked. Vilenov reached down, got his hands full and began to massage. "That's my baby," he breathed. "That's the girl I love." He let go reluctantly, placed Purly's palms on the backs of his thighs, and walked his left hand down her chest while his right hand gently pulled her head forward.

Nicolas Vilenov admired his reflection. Sweat was rolling all down his body. His eyes were glazing. After a minute his right knee began to tremble. He smiled, let his head fall back, and closed his eyes.

Carre placed all his weight on the edge of his left foot, keeping his balance using only two fingertips pressed lightly against the apartment's outer wall. He'd held his breath so long his eyes were popping. Muted, oddly rhythmic sounds came from inside; the sounds of hogs in a dream. He delicately rested his ear on the door, and the hogs took on a distinctly human quality. Except for those muffled grunts and sighs, Purly's apartment was dead quiet. Carre soundlessly exhaled.

His eyes met Vincent Beasely's, raging just across the doorway. Carre's head cocked warningly. He could see Beasely was ready to blow; the man's body language was all profanities—brows knit, nostrils flared, lips drawn back in a snarl. Carre had watched these symptoms grow more pronounced with each passing day, beginning with Beasely's first good long look at a surveillance photo of the suspect, culminating in his yearning, embarrassingly anxious comments about the Purly woman. Now, thanks to their shared hot and cold emotions, the relationship between these officers couldn't have been more electric. Both men were comfortably married, both were immovably principled, and both were irresistibly drawn to Marilyn Jayne Purly. Beasely had it worse: he'd always been, if anything, dedicated to the letter of the law; a soft-spoken cop with a good record. Not the sort of man to lose his head or his heart. Carre was by nature on a tighter rein; stiff, pressed, and polished, and notorious for his ability to take drastic disciplinary measures without a trace of sympathy. Yet, despite Beasely's steady and very unprofessional change, Carre had refused to have him reassigned, had instead become his staunchest supporter. For, from somewhere in his midbrain, Roland Carre hated, hated, *hated* Nicolas Vilenov almost as much as did Vince Beasely.

Carre flicked his head and looked back at the drive. Most of the buildings' tenants were standing in a broad crescent facing Purly's apartment, restrained by three uniformed officers. A man in a white shirt and tie waited at midpoint, staring at an upstairs window. The rest of the tenants were leaning on the twin building's upper rail, watching intently.

All this crowd control should have been unnecessary. The buildings' occupants had proved quite compliant, even shy, timidly filing into their units to peep from windows and cracked doors. There they had remained until only a few minutes ago, when their massive manager began sucking officers into a whispered shouting match over rights and procedures. One by one they had reopened their doors to mill uncertainly between the buildings. The woman became more unruly in their presence, as though readying a charge, but backed off grudgingly when officers threatened her with obstruction. She returned to pacing her assigned perimeter, only to subtly work her way back in as the raid neared the moment of truth.

Carre lowered his left hand until the fingers just graced the doorknob. He pinched it lightly, turned it centimeter by centimeter. The knob was unlocked. He turned it back just as slowly. The chain might be up, but it wouldn't stand against his and Beasely's shoulders.

The coordinating officer's full attention was on the apartment directly above Purly's. In that unit the drapes parted to reveal a dark standing figure. This man turned his head to look back into the room. After a tense half-minute he dropped his arm in a chopping motion, copied instantly by the man on the ground. Carre gently turned the knob. He and Beasely, with a quick exchange of glances, hit the door as one.

What Carre saw stopped him dead. He barely budged when Beasely slammed into him from behind.

Seated at opposite ends of the couch were a clothed man and woman. A tall glass of iced tea stood on a coffee table at their knees. Scattered about this glass were maybe two dozen supermarket coupons and a number of magazines. Carre automatically sampled titles: *SAILBOATING NOW. KITTENS & PUPPIES. POETRY FOR BEGINNERS.* His eyes were drawn to an old black and white TV across the room. On the screen a cartoon whirlwind raced across a cartoon desert.

"Beep beep!" the whirlwind cried.

A black videocassette recorder was perched on the set's console. Carre walked over and stared into the VCR's remote control sensor. For a weird moment he was totally in the dark. He straightened and found himself studying the faded print of a skinny, homely ballerina. As he turned back to face the room his attention seemed to drift along behind.

The suspect was on his feet; every aspect of his expression and posture consistent with surprise and indignation. A cussing Beasely had one arm around his neck, the other twisting his wrist up behind his back. Marilyn Purly, dressed in happy-face muumuu and fuzzy pink slippers, was screaming out of her mind. On an end table were a green rotary telephone and a carefully folded tablecloth. Carre overcame a ridiculous urge to drape this cloth around the screaming woman.

There came a repeated, dreamlike stomping above. The concussions staggered Carre. One moment he thought he would faint, the next his consciousness was struggling with two separate perceptions of a single event: he could have sworn he saw his transparent mirror image reach into a fanny pack to extract something pallid and flaccid. Carre watched dumbstruck as the apparition placed an evidence bag under Purly's chin, signed a document on a clipboard from forensic officer Beloe, and helped the woman undersign. The hallucination blurred, shivered, and passed.

"Marilyn?" Carre managed.

Purly peeked between her fingers and nodded frantically.

"I wonder," Carre's voice said, "if we could step into the kitchen for a minute. You remember me, don't you, Ms. Purly?" She nodded again, languidly now. Carre was absolutely blown away, as though for the first time, by the woman's terrible beauty. A tiny voice in the back of his head begged him not to stare, but he couldn't help it. He took a couple of deep breaths and forced himself to relax. "I'm officer Roland Carre," he said clearly, and with authority. He was back on track. "We had an arrangement to spring a sort of trap on a man suspected of being a serial rapist in the South Bay. You were very cooperative. Does any of this ring a bell with you?"

Purly's head bobbed resignedly. She extended a shaking hand. Carre helped her to her feet and quietly led her into the tiny kitchen, sat her down on one of the cheap little chairs around the cheap little table. He used a thumb to gently peel back an eyelid. Carre saw a red, but otherwise perfectly clear, eyeball.

"Ms. Purly, can you tell me what was taking place before we came in? If you're up to it, that is."

She sobbed and nodded, shivered up and down. "We were having tea. Iced. Nicky and I were discussing catamarans and the migratory patterns of blue whales."

"Nicky?"

Purly giggled spasmodically. "Nicolas," she gushed. "It's my pet name for him." Her expression collapsed, and Carre found himself staring into the flickering baby-blue eyes of an unspeakably frightened woman. His fists clenched. "He...he calls me *Mary Jayne*. No one has ever called me 'Mary Jayne' before."

Carre grasped her shoulders and felt her flesh melt in his hands. He went down on one knee to be face to face. Exercising great control, he said with exaggerated clarity, "Ms. Purly, right before we came in, was this man Nicolas taking advantage of you sexually, or in any manner making you feel afraid for your safety?"

Her reaction was so dramatic Carre had to recoil. Purly tensed up and glared, a lioness protecting her cub. "Certainly not! Nicky is a perfect gentleman!" Plush tears rose under the lids. Suddenly her eyes were rolling in her skull. "What's going on here, officer? What are you doing in my house? Why are you asking these disgusting questions?"

Carre stepped back, his cheeks and ears burning. "I'm very sorry, ma'am. And I deeply appreciate your cooperation."

He stomped into the front room and stood nose-to-nose with Vilenov. Carre's expression underwent a complete transformation, from lovingly sympathetic to jungle-pissed. The breath hissed between his teeth as he fought to retain his professionalism. "One question," he said icily. "Just what the fuck was going on before we blew in here?"

Vilenov winced. Beasely twisted harder.

"Nothing, sir," Vilenov gasped. "Oh, please...nothing! We were talking about boats!" His whole face became contorted. "We were talking about whales, for Christ's sake!"

Slowly the blood drained from Carre's face. When he turned back around, Marilyn Purly was slumped in the kitchen doorway, shivering; a wounded doe in headlights. "Ms. Purly," he said crisply, "I'd like to use your phone, if I may." Without waiting for a reply, he picked up the receiver and dialed Pacific Division. Carre stood facing the wall for a few minutes, his jaw hanging. At last he looked straight up and shook his head in disbelief. He nodded at Beasely.

Beasely cruelly jammed the suspect's arm while whipping out a pair of handcuffs. Vilenov cried out and dropped to his knees. Beasely slapped on the cuffs even as a trio of officers dragged the man back to his feet. "Now pay real close attention," Beasely snarled, his lips right up against Vilenov's ear. "I'm gonna introduce you to Miranda. Oh, I just know you're gonna love meeting her, prick, because we've all seen how interested you are in rights. First off, you've got the right to remain silent. But I've got the right to make you squeal like a pig." Beasely twisted even harder as he shouldered him out the door. Vilenov, protesting all the way, was bullied through a scattering fence of tenants.

Carre turned to face the kitchen doorway. Even bundled in her floppy terrycloth muumuu, Marilyn Purly was the classic damsel in distress, reanimating every guilty fantasy he'd died through since that first interview just outside the black little room. "My work is done here," he said softly. "An officer will arrive shortly to help you get everything sorted out and back to normal. Because of certain inconsistencies, Ms. Purly, I'm requested to assign a crew of specialists. They'll be gathering evidence for a very short while, and I promise you the absolute minimum of inconvenience. It's just that something doesn't make sense here." He ran out of words. Carre dropped back his head and blew out a sigh. "Have a nice day," he whispered, "Mary Jayne," and turned on his heel.

In the apartment directly above, three men were stationed before a long folding table. On this table rested a daisy chain of patched boxes, a computer keyboard, and a large video monitor. The man in charge was seated, his two partners standing close behind his chair. The men were watching the real-time image of Purly sitting topless on the couch, apparently in a trance.

"She looks gone," said the seated man.

"Jesus," whispered the man to his right. "Would you get an eyeful of those! Oh, mama!" Sweat was trickling around his collar. He traded a nervous grin with the man on his left.

It was terribly hot and stuffy in the small apartment. Windows and drapes were sealed for secrecy's sake, fan and air conditioner shut down to preserve the integrity of electronic readings. The sitting man wiped sweat from his eyes and leaned closer to the monitor. He watched Purly step offscreen and return to the couch. Almost as if reading his mind, she slowly turned her head to face the camera. The seated man saw what appeared to be a spark of emotional pain. He tapped a finger repeatedly on a key. The image on the monitor zoomed in to feature Purly's flawless face. He made a quick note on a pad to his right, zoomed the image back to full room.

"Oh, Lord," a voice whispered, as a naked Nicolas Vilenov walked in from the bathroom. Vilenov squeezed between Purly and the coffee table, his back to the camera. The seated man tapped rapidly on the keyboard. A bordered image appeared around the naked man's left arm. A few more taps, and features within the border enlarged. He returned the image to normal. "Menthol something," he said.

"Mentholatum," came a voice behind him.

"Oh…*mama!*"

They watched the man throw his clothes on the table and lather his hands. As he pulled her face forward, the seated man barked, *"Davis!"*

Immediately the man to his left stepped to the window and parted the drapes. He raised his arm and looked back into the room. The two men at the monitor leaned even closer, their heads almost touching. The camera zoomed in, showing only a buttock and most of Purly's face. Her eyes appeared to be made of glass.

"Go!" said the seated man.

The man at the window dropped his arm. When the officer below copied his gesture he released the drapes and crept back to the chair. The three men huddled around the monitor expectantly.

Daylight burst in on the screen's left side. The naked man whirled. One hand covered his eyes, the other his genitals. He tripped backward over the coffee table, but didn't lose his feet.

The two crouching men laughed excitedly, pounding on the chair like a couple of drunken lugs watching the Super Bowl. The long days of whispering and tiptoeing were over. Gone were the endless hours in front of a featureless screen, waiting for Purly to turn on a light…to do *anything*. The men saw Carre and Beasely lunge into the picture. Beasely threw a vicious chokehold on the naked man, while Carre stood watching Purly going through the motions; arms embracing an invisible man, head rolling back and forth. They saw Carre bend down, saw his round brown eye look directly into the camera. Carre turned and walked over to an end table, picked up a folded tablecloth, spread it wide and draped it around the nude woman. The surveillance men groaned.

"No, Rollin'!" cried one of the crouching men, stamping his foot repeatedly. "You're covering up the wrong one!" The man beside him giggled.

Carre pulled a pair of latex gloves from a fanny pack and tugged them on. He then extracted a plastic bag with a gummed label across its face, held this bag under Purly's chin, put an arm over her shoulders, and spoke in her ear. Purly obediently leaned forward and spat. Carre sealed the evidence bag and handed it to Beloe. Beloe produced a clipboard. Carre signed, Beloe countersigned. Carre placed the pen in Purly's cold hand and coached her signature. Beloe took the clipboard and moved out of the picture. Carre helped Purly offscreen into the kitchen. In a minute he reappeared alone. He strode up to the naked man writhing in Beasely's grip.

Carre snarled something and stepped back. The man was forced to put on his clothes, even as Beasely maintained his chokehold. Beasely twisted the man's arm until he lashed back his head to meet his tormentor's eyes, but Beasely, muttering rapidly, kept his cheek pressed right up against his ear. Carre looked to the kitchen and spoke a few words, then stepped to the end table, hesitated. He turned to glare at the suspect.

A black cloud passed over the restrained man's expression. His eyes swept all around the room, out the apartment's doorway and back inside. For just a second they seemed to look straight into the camera's lens. All three surveillance men shuddered involuntarily.

Carre, facing away from the camera, dialed a number and spoke to the wall. He replaced the receiver, stared hard at the ceiling and shook his head incredulously. He looked to his left and nodded.

Vincent Beasely savagely twisted Vilenov's arm while whipping out handcuffs. Vilenov went straight down. Three officers swarmed onscreen and roughly hauled him to his feet. The knot of prisoner and officers moved offscreen into the wall of light. Roland Carre stepped out of the picture.

"Okay," said the seated man. "Show's over." With nervous exchanges, the two standing agents signed out on a clipboard and went jostling outside. The man in the chair tweaked the monitor's image, made a number of observations on the legal pad by his elbow.

But his eyes never left the screen.

Chapter Two

Abram

The man staring through the observation window was standing so still he might have been a cardboard cutout. The shatterproof glass of this window, as broad as the corridor's facing wall, permitted booking officers, as well as lockdown officers, to make out every detail in the boxcar-shaped visitation room. Inside were a steel table and bench, a pay phone, and a smallish, dark-haired man in Levis, loafers, and light blue long-sleeved shirt. He was sitting perfectly still with his forearms resting on his knees, deep in thought.

Lawrence Abram's eyes narrowed. The prisoner pretty much matched the impression he'd given over the phone; a contentious, physically and morally repellent character in his upper thirties, of East European descent. Even in half-profile there was something disturbing about the eyes.

"All right," Abram said softly. "I'm ready." The guard stepped around him and unlocked the door.

Nicolas Vilenov didn't jump up as the famous defense attorney entered the room, didn't gush with greeting and gratitude. His expression remained a spiteful scowl, but those peculiar eyes became quite focused. Abram felt an instinctive contempt for the man. It was the hardest thing in the world to recover his trademark geniality, but he smiled and extended a hand. The diamond winked on his pinky, the Rolex peeped from a silk sleeve.

Vilenov offered a limp hand. At its touch the sense of contempt came back a hundredfold. Abram was aware of a real sense of anger and resentment. Unbidden, an all but forgotten word returned to him. *Incubus*, he thought, and released the hand.

There was an unpleasant pause.

Abram said, "Mr. Vilenov, when my secretary accepted your sole allotted phone call, her first inclination was to put you on what we call 'the elevator.' The elevator places a caller on hold for eternity, while canned Muzak dumbs him into the ozone. Eventually he's so anaesthetized by insipid recorded garbage he forgets his imaginary dragon and returns to the couch whence he came. However, Dottie said there was 'something' in your voice. I've worked with her for seventeen years, and have come to trust her like a lover. Now, I don't generally conduct business on the strength of a call divulging a public storage locker's combination, but it was a relatively slow day, the locker's location was very near my office, and curiosity got the better of me. *Or*," he said, trying the light touch, "maybe there *was* 'something' in your voice." Vilenov glared. "At any rate," Abram went on uncomfortably, "I discovered the locker did indeed hold sufficient cash—and then some—to retain my services. After removing a sample from the site, I reorganized my schedule around this interview but, because of ethical concerns, undertook a number of preliminary checks. The thoroughness of my investigation will explain, in part, why I've arrived so late in the day. In the first place, the money turned out to be unmarked."

"It's all clean," Vilenov muttered. "Save your energy."

Abram popped open his briefcase. Resting on parallel stacks of loose pages was a paper-clipped fan of bills, ranging from tens on the left to hundreds on the right, like a hand of cards. The bills were not new or well kept.

"Here's your money, Mr. Vilenov. I want you to be aware from the outset that your property is in order."

Vilenov didn't bother to look. "It's yours, man. That, and all you can spend. I'm prepared to make you a very rich man, Mr. Abram, just as soon as you get the job done."

"And that job is?"

"To spring me immediately, and to clear me of any and all charges."

Abram watched a prisoner being processed. "That's pretty cut and dry." After a minute he said, still staring out the wide window, "You, sir, are at this point what is known as a cipher. There's no law against possessing so much cash, but it certainly doesn't make your case look less suspect." He turned back. "We don't even have an address on you. Were you living under a bridge?"

"I use hotels, and I always pay in cash. Is that okay with you? Is there any law saying a man has to have a permanent address?"

"None whatsoever. I'm just trying to learn what I can about a prospective client. If we're going to work together, I think it would be a good idea for us to be on the same side." Abram clasped his hands behind his back and again looked outside. "After I visited your locker I headed back to my office and got busy on the phone. Finding information about you was like looking for water in the Mojave. According to every indication you are unemployed, do not file tax returns, and have not hit the lottery. Believe me, if you had a traceable real income the I.R.S. would know all about you. So unless you're a very successful bank robber, a gun runner or dope dealer, I'm stumped. Have you been stashing money in a mattress all your life for just this eventuality? Have you found buried treasure? You'll forgive my prying, but it's not a matter of idle curiosity. I command high figures in my practice, and my clients are, as a rule, most accountable in their finances. But you, sir, as I said, are a cipher. An independently wealthy individual for whom a fairly thorough records check reveals no birth certificate, no social security number, no medical history, no rap sheet…the only documentation of your existence is a newly confiscated California ID card, demonstrated through a simple check with the DMV to be a quality street forgery." Abram paused as Vilenov hawked and spat on the floor. The attorney scowled. "Excuse me, but I never got a spoken pronunciation, just Dottie's scribble. Is it *Vile*, or something closer to *Villain*?"

The prisoner's stare was so hard Abram had to look away. "My name is Nicolas Vilenov. Vi-*len*-ahv, if that pleases you. Or, better: V'*len*-of. Don't worry. You'll get used to it quick enough.

"And as to my money, chew on this: I inherited it from my father, a Romanian immigrant who passed away in California. I am hiring you, the famous Mr. Lawrence Abram, to represent me in what has the potential to become, in my life, an absolute catastrophe. What part of the above escapes you?"

"There isn't a whole lot about you that doesn't escape me. But you yourself, Mr. Vilenov, have missed quite a bit." Abram exhibited an erect forefinger. "Allow me to delineate the sequence of events leading to your present incarceration.

"First off, it seems that a number of weeks ago the landlady of Ms. Purly's building, a Helga Scarboro, became highly suspicious of your dealings with her tenant."

Vilenov rolled his neck, leaned back down, stared at the floor. "I know the witch," he muttered.

"Yes. Apparently she had an ongoing altercation with you, adamantly claiming you had drugged and raped her tenant, a beautiful and helpless young woman with a history of violent self-abuse. This landlady's defense of her lodger is undoubtedly selfish: Marilyn Purly's tenancy is subsidized through monthly Social Security Insurance checks, direct-deposited into Scarboro's account and guaranteed in perpetuity so long as Purly remains unable to provide for herself. At any rate, Scarboro got the rest of her boarders into a group and had them sign a petition claiming you were making a practice of taking the Purly woman against her will. Even though Purly at first refused to go along, Scarboro photocopied the petition and began circulating it throughout the neighborhood, to the media, to her congressman. She badgered Pacific Division to no end, and finally the division commander assigned a team to place you under surveillance. Over the course of the next two weeks you were tailed and photographed extensively. There are photos of you checking into various hotels for the night, dining alone, walking on the beach. If you boarded a bus, a man was dispatched to board at a stop farther on to continue the surveillance. You were followed wherever you went. And there are photographs of you paying visits to the homes of no less than eleven different women over those two weeks. All these women fit what Pacific's men colloquially define as 'drop-dead gorgeous.' Yet, strange to say, none are married or romantically involved. They live quiet, lonesome lives, hold unglamorous jobs. They're spinsters, before their time. All were interviewed by detectives, and not one had any recollection of a male visitor, but, upon viewing full-face surveillance photographs, each reacted with high emotion, in a manner the detectives described as expressing a range from repugnance to horror. Upon viewing shots of your entering or exiting their premises, these women, as a rule, went right into hysterics."

Vilenov shook his head slowly, looking more bored than offended.

"Having gained these ladies' permission," Abram went on, "their places of residence were forensically sampled. And it was determined, as in the case of Ms. Purly's apartment, that these residences were all littered with semen deposits, foreign hairs, fingerprints, tracks—you name it. Somebody, whether the good ladies knew it or not, had been very busy.

"The inconclusiveness and rising hysteria—there were two nervous breakdowns right in Pacific Division—prompted a videotaping of Ms. Purly's apartment. After much cajoling from her landlady, Purly agreed to go along with the setup; to be the bait, if you will. A police technician disguised as a television repairman rewired Purly's VCR and implanted a camera, its lens positioned behind the remote control sensor's window. Surveillance equipment was tapped into the unit's coaxial cable, and the apartment was observed, and videotaped, from the vacated apartment directly above.

"Abram observed Vilenov narrowly. "The surveillance crew captured on videotape someone, who certainly appears to be you, receiving fellatio from Marilyn Jayne Purly. Purly maintains zero recollection of the event." He raised a hand. "One of the members of this surveillance crew is trained to observe individuals for signs of intoxication, mental retardation, or any inability to respond defensively. It was this man's professional opinion that Purly was totally out of it, and incapable of self-will. He had a man give the go-ahead to officers below. These agents then burst in and found…nothing."

"She unlocked the door," Vilenov snarled. "The bitch

set me up!"

For some reason Vilenov's display of rancor created an abrupt mood shift. Abram's expression twisted nastily, his intended word of caution erupting as a bark bordering on assault. "*Please*, Mr. Vilenov! Save your whining accusations for therapy!" Abram just as quickly apprehended himself, and after a hard half-minute continued with forced civility, "Besides, if anybody has some explaining to do it's the commander at Pacific, who, uncharacteristically, didn't have the self-control to pull out at the climax, so to speak." He removed his glasses from a vest pocket and consulted his notebook. "Roland Carre, senior officer at the scene, told the commander over Purly's phone that the premises were clear of any overt criminal activity—informed him, in essence, that two weeks of surveillance and setup were a bust, that the claimants' reports were a lot of hooey, that the monitoring specialists were all full of it, and that every man involved in the investigation, himself included, was an amateurish paranoiac in an expensive parade of fools." Abram returned the glasses to his vest. "This might have been a bit much to swallow at one sitting. At any rate, Carre was reamed over the phone; was told to clean the crap out of his eyes and make the arrest, was told if he wanted to keep his job he'd better get busy and gather every scrap of evidence he could get his incompetent little hands on. Carre immediately assigned a team to the site, and that team was striking gold long before Dottie got your call.

"Oh, and one other thing:

"Purly earlier agreed to help collect a semen sample. At Parker Center that sample now awaits comparison with samples taken from the eleven sites aforementioned. The Purly sample was seized in conjunction with an affidavit—signed on the scene by Purly, a forensic man, and Carre…although not a one professes any recollection of so doing."

"*Bitch!*"

In the corridor a cuffed prisoner whirled on his transporting officer. The two went down biting and kicking, quickly swarmed by deputies. Abram stepped to the window and watched, strangely excited. When he turned back to Vilenov his eyes were burning.

"Therein lies the rub. My investigation took me promptly to the District Attorney's office, where I went over a copy of the videotape with Mr. Prentis, and discussed the details of your capture and the lack of pertinent records. The DA, Mr. Vilenov, simply has no eyewitness corroboration to any of this. Nothing is conclusive here. Tests for room toxicity were taken immediately. A whiskey bottle and an open jar of ointment were seized, along with an array of smut books and exactly three hundred and seventy dollars in loose cash. The contents of the refrigerator and medicine cabinet, water from the tap…even the air was sampled. Results so far, to the best of my knowledge, are all negative, and the discrepancy between visual and video remains a mystery." He looked down his nose. "Item: you were filmed by the security camera at Barry's Liquor half an hour prior to the raid. The tape shows you in a transaction with the clerk involving liquor, magazines, and what looks like most of the drawer. The owner calls Santa Monica police saying he's been robbed by the clerk, who claims no memory of you or the incident." Abram shrugged. "Ms. Purly's apartment was quickly cordoned off for further analysis, leaving only a narrow corridor connecting rooms, so that she could continue living there as compensation for her assistance in this investigation. She reportedly made a beeline for her *very black* bedroom immediately upon Carre's departure, and there remains barricaded, quiet as a mouse. My personal impression is that Marilyn Jayne Purly is an incorrigibly disturbed woman."

"Abram," Vilenov said with a throwaway glance, "her distress is only beginning."

"How so?"

The prisoner stood up, sat right back down. He shook his head in frustration. "Just get me out of here, okay? And take all the money you need. You and your good buddy the DA can split it down the middle for all I care."

Abram squared his shoulders. "I'm going to pretend I didn't hear that." He took a deep breath and unclenched his fists. "Mr. Vilenov, I don't have the power to arbitrarily orchestrate your release. And as for the DA being my friend, well, that doesn't make him some kind of crony."

Vilenov rolled his eyes to the ceiling. "Strikes me as sort

of funny that a defense lawyer and a district attorney should be so buddy-buddy, that's all." Again he spat on the floor.

"Your manners aren't exactly winning me over, either."

Vilenov shrugged.

Abram tapped his nails on the table. "Look, we weren't always so close. Or maybe we were too close. You're aware of my work as a prosecutor?"

"But money talks, huh, Mr. ex-Prosecutor?"

Abram glared. "With lucidity," he said softly.

Vilenov rose and began to pace, but halted after only a few steps. With his head down and his fists stuffed in his pockets, he addressed Abram as though the attorney were a child.

"Now don't you worry about your precious fee, Mr. Abram. That locker holds just a pinch. I've got cash stashed all over this city, and I can get more any time I feel like it. Lovely, lovely money. More than you can spend, more than you can count, more pretty green paper than you've ever even *dreamed* of caressing."

"Really! You've certainly got my undivided attention now, Mr. Vilenov. I'm intrigued."

"So you just get my ass *out* of here, *now*, and later on you and I'll walk hand in hand into court, and you can flash that famous Lawrence Abram smile. We're going to need it. I'm telling you, man, this is only the tip of the iceberg. You're going to be hearing from a slew of…ex-girlfriends."

"And *why*, Mr. Vilenov, would all these women wait so long?"

"Be-*cause*, Mr. Abram, an individual, in the flesh, can produce certain…effects…that can't be generated by a simple two-dimensional representation."

Abram raised an eyebrow. "Are you hinting you've been threatening women, and that these women will only identify you in person? Meaning, in custody?"

"No! You don't understand; it's way more complicated than that. They can only identify me when I'm *not* around them." Vilenov cocked his head, affronted. "You know what, Abram? I'm not really sure I approve of your tone. 'Threatening women,' indeed. What's that supposed to mean, dude? Like, I can't get my way without resorting to intimidation or something?" He smiled vaguely. "Good-looking women are just fruit on my tree. They're plums for the plucking, Abram, and I'm not ashamed to say I'm one hell of a plucker."

Abram was speechless, his expression uglier than he knew. His appreciation of propriety, in this one short half hour, had been violated in ways that should have filled a lifetime. In the thundering silence he whispered, with barely contained venom, "I'm sure Marilyn Purly, if she had a voice in the matter, would be first to agree."

Vilenov exploded. "Just get me out of here! All right? Get me out, get me out, *get me out!* You're pissing me off, man! Use your connections, use your charm. Use my money. Just get on with it!"

Abram raised a warning forefinger. *"Use your money?"* But halfway to Vilenov's nose the gesture was preempted. His arm fell to his side, dead from the elbow down. Abram forced a few deep breaths, suddenly clammy in his armpits and crotch. When he spoke again his tone was borderline-conciliatory.

"What *you* don't understand, Mr. Vilenov, is that my reputation was gained over many years of playing by the book. I earned my stripes through hard work, not through hard cash. And I'm no simple bail bondsman. As I've been *trying* to explain, my investigation included a lengthy dialogue with the District Attorney, who is, understandably, in no great hurry to see you back on the street."

"I know all about your big bad childhood pal Nelson Prentis," Vilenov said sourly. "Dueling comrades, battling buddies. Right now I'm the wrong cat to lay that Butch and Sundance bullshit on; your relationship has been the movie of the week for too many years to count. So do me a favor, man. Don't rewind the same old reel."

That *really* stung; you could call Abram every name in the book, but no one could demean his family or friends. Vilenov was playing with fire here. Although he was still able to comport himself in a manner generations above Vilenov's level, the attorney's calling-out retort came like the snap of a whip. "Apparently, *pal*, you've got one hell of a lot to learn about—"

"Just get me out of here! Okay? Because you're really starting to bug me, man. Get me out *now*, Abram! Not tomor-

row. Not fifteen minutes from now. *Now!* Look, I'm not *ask*ing you, I'm *tell*ing you. *I'm paying you,* for Christ's sake!"

"Everything isn't about money! People in this country can't just buy their way out of legal problems, regardless of what you may have seen in the movies. The I.N.S. is going to want a crack at you, because from the look of things there's absolutely nothing to show you're in this country legally. Various departments of health are going to be interested in you, *sir*. Are you H.I.V. positive? Are you a vector? Mr. Vilenov, there are sexual predation claims of an egregious nature to investigate. What kind of system would just casually release such a suspect? Also, there's a great deal of cash to be accounted for. I haven't told a soul, mind you, but I'll guarantee you the ball is already in motion. Detective work has a way of discovering bits and pieces, both peripherally and by extrapolation, about even the most discreet individual. A person in your position, Mr. Vilenov—if that truly is your name—has to go through channels, has to jump through hoops…and has to *wait*. I'm telling you right now, there's just no way in hell you're going to get out of here without first running a very tight legal gauntlet, no matter who's representing you. Not even if you've got a pass from God Almighty."

Vilenov looked around the room and smiled cockily. "Look, I can walk out any time I want, so don't patronize me. And quit trying to spook me with all your legal mumbo-jumbo. People do what I want—always have, always will. And they always remember me in a positive light, no matter what went down. That's if I want them to remember me at all. I can move men, Mr. Abram, and I can make women. I can do any bitch I please; upright, on all fours, or spread-eagled, and I can make her perform *just* the way I like." He let his head fall, and in that instant Abram thought he saw the man's eyes blaze with a frustration beyond words. He waited. At last Vilenov mumbled, "It's a gift." A thought struck him and he looked back up. "You're a bright boy, Abram. What do you know about pheromones?"

"What's that got to do with anything?"

"It's got everything to do with everything."

The attorney cocked his head and squinted at a tiny

smudge on the ceiling. "Biochemistry," he said, pinching the bridge of his nose. "Hormones that induce same-species reactions. Very subtle. Glandular emanations, traceable in sweat, urine, breath." He waved a hand irritably. "Chemistry was not my strong suit."

"Too bad. You might have learned something."

Abram scowled. "Been spreading your musk around town, have you? Well…guess what: I didn't sleep all the way through classes. No microscopic secretion can produce a direct physical reaction. Your imagination's running away with you."

"My imagination is firmly ensconced in reality, Abram. I'm not talking about secretions; that's crowd stuff. I'm talking about a focalized force, an adaptive influence established in maybe one in a billion people."

"Keep dreaming."

"It's no fantasy. All I need is eye contact, and this whole silly-ass species will carry out my blackest wishes without hesitation…even without my bidding. I can make anybody eat right out of my hand. And I can do it with or without your fancy reputation."

"You don't say! Now I'm *really* intrigued!" Abram rapped on the wall. "But before you unleash your fabulous dark legions, just how do you propose to effect this awesome escape? Melt the walls? Break through bulletproof glass? Or is Scotty above us somewhere, all set to beam you up?"

"No, funny man. Like I said, I can walk out."

"Of course you can. So the next logical question would have to be: what are you waiting for? And why do you need me?"

"*Because*, Mr. Abram," Vilenov said exasperatedly, "there are now full-face photographs in the DA's possession, and forensic samples in Parker Center. I need to get my hands on those samples *fast*, before a real case can be built against me. And the last thing I need is my picture all over the evening news. So it behooves me to make a legal exit; I don't want to skip out of here as the bogeyman. Now, you're *going* to arrange my immediate release. And if my face gets on TV you're *going* to stand behind me, and sue the goddamned media if you have to. Then you're *going* to work to clear my name so that I may walk around a free man again."

"Mr. Vilenov...*should I choose* to represent you I will, at the minimum, guarantee you that in less than seventy-two hours you will be a 'free man' again. And if you're really all that camera-shy—"

"I don't *have* seventy-two hours!"

"Sir! *Please!* You cannot be held forever! You are incarcerated under hearsay. You are here solely because the investigation's commanding officer authorized your arrest over the phone on the word of a surveillance specialist, who determined, via an electronic medium, that you were committing rape. And the man saddled with the job of resolving this quagmire already knows he hasn't got a leg to stand on."

"Your buddy. Nelson Prentis."

"My counterpart. The District Attorney. Mr. Prentis is aware you've been placed behind bars without cause, and realizes your release is imminent. As I keep *trying* to explain, you are, right now, being held for a variety of ulterior reasons—a murky mess which can and will be cleared by patience and application." He glanced at his watch. "Mr. Vilenov, the DA is the county's top prosecutor, and I am, if I may be so bold, the county's top defense attorney. In any case built against you the burden will be on the prosecution, not the defense. So *relax*. I'm going to work this out with Mr. Prentis, I promise you."

Vilenov sneered, nastily and pugnaciously. "You guys just leave me a few bucks for cab fare, all right?" His eyes glinted.

For a moment Lawrence Abram saw red. When his mind had cleared he said, quietly, "I think this interview's gone on just about long enough."

Vilenov nodded. "Me too." He looked directly into Abram's eyes and the attorney almost fainted. "So this is what's going to happen, Abram. You're *going* to accept my generous cash offer, and you're *going* to attain my immediate release. You *will* represent me in this matter so that I am quickly cleared of any and all charges, and so that my name and face are not open to public censure. I will be able to move about freely. You are going to begin preparing my case, pronto. And that means all your other clients can just go to hell. You'll *get* your facts, and you'll *do* your interviews, and you'll *make* my defense rock-solid. You'll get on the tube and let everybody know that these claims are all bullshit, man, pure bullshit. You're going to profess my innocence. Right? You are about to devote every ounce of your time, talent, and energy to making me look *good.* If your pal the DA gets on my back, you're gonna jump right in his face. *I'm* your buddy now!" Vilenov rolled the tension from his neck while Abram fried. "So you'll be smart. But you'll play dumb if you have to. You won't have enough good things to say about me, *Larry.* Additionally, I am authorizing you to pull from that locker whatever funds you deem necessary. Okay? *Necessary* is the operative word here. *My* money is for *my* defense—not for your leisure. So you just keep your fat sticky lawyerly hands clean! Don't test me on this, man; don't even think about it. You've been warned. Should the locker's working capital become exhausted I will direct you to another site. But understand this: *you* are working for *me.* After this is all over you won't have to like me, or care if I live or die. But for right now you and I are, as you so succinctly put it, 'on the same side.' *Got it?* "

With those final two syllables Abram felt his back slammed against the cold brick wall. His hands found the table's edge and gradually pulled him forward. He swayed before the prisoner, sweat rolling down his face.

Vilenov studied him dispassionately for a while. Finally he drooped his head between his knees and spat. "Now go on, legal boy. Pull some strings. Call your chummy-ass pal and get me the hell out of here."

While Vilenov's head was lowered Abram slammed shut his eyes and turned his back on the man. "Pluck you!" he snarled, and before the wave of primitive fury could drag him under cried, *"Guard!"*

The door instantly swung inward. Vilenov was seized and led cursing from the room. Abram steadied himself against the stainless steel table, waiting for the stampede of savage emotions to subside. He would not reopen his eyes. Clenching his teeth, he slapped his palms against the wall, felt his way to the pay phone, and began fishing through his pockets for change.

The swaggering deputy made a point of banging the gate as he entered the cell house, all set to show the loudmouthed prisoner just who was who. In this particularly virile profession, this particularly short, skinny, and pigeon-breasted deputy boldly bore, in addition to his unimposing physical stature, the compound curse of a freckly face, buck teeth, jug ears, and overall cherubic expression. His compensatory scowl and blustering manner only worked against him, so he scowled a little deeper, stomped a little harder.

"*Hey* you, now just you chill out in there! Now, I *mean* it. You got me? You just stop all that darned hollering, buddy, or you're gonna wind up with something to *really* holler about!"

Vilenov glared through the bars, and the deputy mellowed at once. Three other prisoners in the cell house—two bald, heavy-set, highly tattooed Latino gang members and a burly, bearded bar fighter—sat quietly on a stainless steel bench against the wall.

"Why am I still in here?" Vilenov demanded. "Where's my attorney? Where's Lawrence Abram?"

"I'm…not sure, sir."

"Well…*go find out!*"

The deputy rang out the gate and reappeared in ten minutes. Vilenov was pacing the cell house, in and out of the wide-open individual cells. The moment the gate was open he stopped pacing and gored the deputy with his eyes.

"Sir, you've," the little deputy stammered, "sir, you've been ordered held indefinitely, sir. Sir, there's no sign of Mr. Abram, sir." He stood slouched at an angle, perspiring heavily and sniffling.

Once Vilenov had renewed his pacing the deputy slunk back out, gently shutting the gate behind him. After a while Vilenov turned to meet his three cellmates' eyes. As if cued, they slid down the bench, pressed tightly together. Vilenov sat on the vacated space, rested his chin on his locked hands, and began to think.

Chapter Three

Prentis

Abram was all-in by the time he made it home Sunday night. The family had spent the weekend in a very pricey Big Bear lakeside cabin: Abram, a drunken bundle of post-interview nerves, had recklessly outbid a group of contractors over the Internet. The isolation and gorgeous view did little to placate him; all over that weekend he was plagued by inexplicable feelings of persecution, by bouts of anger, by creeping malaise. But once in the womb of family, he hadn't touched a drop.

Traffic on the long drive back had moved at a crawl, the 405 coming out of the Valley being socked in, predictably, clear to Sunset. Compounding Abram's misery were his wife's on-again, off-again headaches, Archie the golden Lab's delayed reaction to a tentative roadkill snack, and the kids' insistence on playing ad nauseam a newly released cutesy pop CD. So his first move home was to head for the basement office, where he pulled a Tupperware thermos and chilled glass from the little Post-it-peppered refrigerator. In the thermos was pre-mixed Piña Colada, his self-prescribed sedative and sole mood enhancer. He automatically rewound his answering machine; Abram got a lot of calls even on weekends and holidays.

The first message was a request from Nelson Prentis for a call back. Abram fast forwarded. The requests became increasingly urgent. When he felt somewhat relaxed he set down his glass and dialed the DA's home phone. The anxious voice broke in halfway through the first ring. "Larry?"

"I got your messages, Nelson. All of 'em."

"Where in Christ have you been? Our man's escaped from the del Rey substation."

Abram sighed explosively. For a moment his skull was socked in by cement. He pushed himself forward in his chair and very steadily drained his glass. Though hairs were standing on the back of his neck, his voice was nonchalant. "Well, well. I'll be damned. How did he do it?" Every aspect of his attention was now focused solely on his right eardrum.

"That's what I want to know, that's what everybody wants to know. Damn you, Larry, that's what I've been calling all weekend for!" Prentis matched his friend's sigh. "Out with it! What happened during your little in-house interview?"

Abram tried to let go. But how to describe that extraordinary meeting and still come off as a rational observer...and just why in hell should it be anybody else's business, anyway? He was aware of a real resentment, of a spark of rage, even— but Prentis was his best friend; they'd always shared information. Abram shivered as if a cup of ice water had just been poured down his back. Being evasive would only arouse suspicion. Tell the man what he wants to know, and nothing else. Tread lightly and spin well. Abram pressed his lips against the mouthpiece, details of the interview becoming increasingly fuzzy as he spoke. Gradually his voice took on the tenor of a monotone. And the farther he allowed his mind to drift, the drier that monotone grew. "Well...I spoke with him a while, tried to get some background. He's a really decent guy, Nellie; good sense of humor, easy to talk to. We chatted a bit about the Angels and Dodgers, just to loosen up, but he kept going back to his feelings about the poor and homeless in Venice, and how he'd like to make a real difference, if only he could. He even recited some of his quasi-utopian poetry for me; nothing groundbreaking, but definitely heartfelt. There's a real optimist in there, buddy. Anyhow, I've accepted his offer of a cash retainer, so as soon as he's back in custody I'll be representing him."

"About that cash—"

Abram sat bolt-upright. "I haven't spent it, haven't banked it, haven't touched it! Okay? And I'm not about to divulge its whereabouts. Mr. Vilenov told me he was feeling particularly harassed, and needed someone he could trust." He wiped his brow with a sleeve. "Anyway, I can tell you it's unmarked, and in all denominations."

"Now hold on a minute, Larry. When you called me on Friday you were all over the place. Remember? You kept yapping about how urgent it was to clear this guy, and we never did get around to the money's origins. You wanted me to understand what a *nice* guy he was, and how very *important* it was that he be released *immediately*. Jesus. You begged me to talk to the Chief, then to go to the mayor. You even asked me to lean on the station. You worked in every argument you knew before appealing directly, and shamelessly, to the strength of our friendship. What a daft speech." Abram could almost feel Prentis shaking his head with amusement. "You must've been drunk off your ass, buddy."

With the sudden relaxation in tension Abram's entire body crashed, leaving him limp and spent in his chair. He tried to jog his memory. It was like poking a bruise. "I...I don't remember a whole lot about that conversation, Nellie. Just you getting hot."

"Don't call me like that at the office again, period. Enough said. So. Where did you go after you hung up?"

"I had to get away, Nelson, and fast. Don't ask me why. You know the family does Big Bear twice a year. I decided to make it three times this year."

"Okay, my friend. That gap is filled. Now for the sixty-four thousand dollar question—and same as always: totally off the record. I'll concede to keeping the money's whereabouts your little secret. Just tell me, Larry. *Tell* me. How does some guy off the street, with no social security card and no visible means of support, acquire the cash to hire one of the county's top defense attorneys? Come on, already. Give."

Abram's features twitched and his voice again waxed monotonic. His eyes slowly glazed while his mind dealt out words and images in real time. His flat, nearly unbroken speech was occasionally punctuated by increasingly skeptical *"Mm-hmm!"*'s from his friend.

"Said it was his father's legacy. Apparently papa didn't

trust banks. The old man was a local salvager and handyman who humped like a dog day and night, saving all he could. He stashed this cash away for over twenty years, working himself right into the grave in the process. Told the boy its location on his deathbed. Ever since, Mr. Vilenov's lived frugally in the South Bay, eking out his means by sleeping on the beach and accepting a meal every now and then at St. John's. He works off and on, sweeping up and such, for small cash, but he's never had bona fide, gainful employment. He also scavenges for cans and bottles around the Marina, making a few bucks a day. Let's see now...what else? Well, he likes Jesus and small animals, sailboats and roller skates. Never married, no dependents. He was totally in the dark about the Purly incident, and blushed like a schoolgirl when I explained the charges in depth.

"It seems Purly took pity on him one day, when she found him shivering in his old sleeping bag on the beach. She hired him, out of kindness, to do small jobs around her apartment, and let him use her shower once a week. She cooked his meals, sewed up his tattered old jeans. It gave her purpose, Nelson. Eventually a friendship grew around their common needs, though it never progressed beyond the platonic. He's way too shy. All the same, he feels very protective toward her."

There was a long pause. Abram tapped on the mouthpiece, wondering if the line was dead.

"Larry," came the DA's careful voice. "You and I are not talking about the same guy here."

"I interviewed him, Nelson. Not you."

"So you did. But the man I'm discussing is a fugitive, has been filmed receiving fellatio from a completely confused woman, and has, on looks alone, launched a reign of terror among the South Bay's female population."

Abram whistled softly and pulled at his drink. *Ron Rico rum, light. Very tropical, very soothing.* "That's some pretty tough stuff, Nelson. Sure he's a fugitive. But the real issue here is station security, right? You yourself said you don't have the slightest. If I'd been jailed without cause proper, and I was scared, and somebody left the gate open, well...I might walk too. I don't know."

"He's *still* a fugitive. And there were a total of six other prisoners detained at the time of his disappearance, none nearly as charming as you make your boy out to be. For some reason they're all still in custody."

"And how do these gentlemen account for Mr. Vilenov's absence?"

"They can't. They don't have the foggiest."

Abram snorted. "So there you go. They don't know, you don't know, I don't know. What do you want from me?"

"A little insight, Larry. For instance, there's the very graphic video evidence of a man suspected of being a serial rapist, caught on camera in the act of sodomizing a woman—"

"Marilyn Purly is not a witness to anything! She's a total space case. And the taped evidence we went over prior to my interview with Mr. Vilenov is inadmissible and wholly inconclusive, and you know it. Even were it admissible, how would we establish just whose ugly butt that was? How could we be certain those people on the tape are not actors, and the front room not a set?"

"The tape is a live recording, not a dupe. You know that. And why wait until now to bring this up? What's happening to you, man?"

"Nelson, this whole thing is bogus! What proof can you offer that a pre-recorded tape wasn't inserted and its signal exported to your surveillance equipment?" Abram's smile was pugilistic. "Nelson, old buddy, old pal o' mine, how in the world do you plan to elicit testimony from a site where all who were present can't remember a thing?"

"Ah, Jesus."

"Give me a break, Mr. Prosecutor. You don't usually reach like this. Oh—and what was that other little thing? A panic in the city? Vilenov runs amok?"

Abram could hear the DA's fingertips drumming on his broad oak desk. "Let me guess, Larry. A couple of 'Coladas?"

"Just the one," Abram said, reaching for the thermos. "Make that two. It's still the weekend." He filled his glass. "But seriously, what were you saying about a scare?"

"Haven't you turned on the TV? Can't you find a newspaper rack?"

"Like I told you, I've been camping."

"Okay then. Let me fill you in. After Vilenov escaped, every man at that station was disemboweled, yet not one claimed to have a clue. They've all been relieved, and an interim crew set up in their place. Right off the bat that turned out to be a bad idea; the new man in charge didn't handle the transition at all well. He allowed shit to slip through that the regulars at del Rey would never let get by. That station's solid, and proud of it. And even as this new man's busy tucking in butts, a bunch of innocuous little events are turning the mess into a disaster.

"Seems this fellow tenant of Purly's, a Frederick Mars, called Channel 5 on the day of Vilenov's arrest. He felt your prospective client was getting a raw deal by being set up. Mars was the sole hold-out in that tenants' committee I told you about. An intern at Channel 5, one Miss Chica Hernandez, took Mars's phone call and got her hands on the station's copy of the committee's petition. Smelling a story, she starts making phone calls."

"So what did Mars see that made him—"

"Wait. It gets better. Turns out Chica's boyfriend is a junior deputy temping at the Marina substation, and this deputy leaks that there's a shakeup because of an escape. He only knows it was some spooky guy brought into custody that day, but Chica puts two and two together, and drives out to see her boyfriend on his break. Here the details get a bit fuzzy, but it's certain that intrepid little Chica somehow got a look at Vilenov's mug shot, popped a camera out of her purse during a distraction, and sashayed into 5's studio with a full-face snapshot of Vilenov. The station ran the shot with a byline by Chica herself on the six o'clock, and by six-fifteen the station was so inundated with phone calls they had to bring in extra operators.

"It turns out that Vilenov, Larry, is no stranger to a whole lot of people, nearly all of them women. By seven o'clock every TV station, every radio talk show, and every newspaper was fielding reports of past abuses. The L.A. media are absolutely infatuated with the man who's come to be known as 'The Houdini-rapist'."

Abram picked up his TV's remote unit, switched on the set and hit the mute button.

Immediately the ice-cold visage of Nicolas Vilenov slammed him back in his chair. It was like taking a spike in the forehead. He switched channels. This time a talking head had center stage, and the booking photo was in an upper right-hand corner inset. He tried another channel. Vilenov, full screen. He clicked again. Vilenov. Abram began surfing channels rapidly, and Vilenov's face became a magic lantern image, animated by his leaping thumb. The screen's erratic details were incorporated into a jerky blur; all that remained constant were Vilenov's steady, piercing eyes. Abram hit the off button. Though the screen instantly went dark, two pale gray orbs lingered in the field. The orbs dimmed and passed.

"Larry?"

"I'm here, Nelson."

"By eight o'clock that evening Purly's apartment complex is a rubberneck's Mecca, and everybody who couldn't make the party is at home glued to the tube; primed, reamed, and ready for the next player in their chain of fascination. Enter the dragon.

"This particular reptile steps on stage as the buildings' landlady—a great beast of a woman who insists all queries concerning 'her property' and 'her people' be directed solely to Her. Larry, she's the security guard from Hell; partitioning the public, eyeballing everybody, demanding credentials. The media love her. She's got this carnival-like, palm reader quality. A born storyteller. And when she gets on TV—this big fat woman with all the braids and the gestures and the eighteen pounds of junk jewelry—the camera just can't get enough of her. She starts right off with tales of the macabre; you know the sort: porch bulbs flickering, demonic laughter, black cats arching and hissing, and anybody with ten minutes and a television is mesmerized. Next morning, Saturday, she sets up this big table with a black and gold zodiacal tablecloth, right in front of her apartment by the sidewalk. Suddenly you'd think you were at Woodstock. The nonstop weekend flow is a nightmare for law enforcement, but it's this landlady's fifteen minutes, and she knows that so long as she's on her own property she's free to make the most of it. She's a canny one, Larry. Right after this whole big scene broke she was approached with options for T-shirts and mugs and the like, but she knew she had to keep face. So the old fraud claimed she was above making a quick buck, swearing her only object was to exorcize her buildings. Apparently she covertly employed a concessions manager, because that same afternoon her wares were popping up all over the place. And once reporters went after her puppet tenants she jumped right on them. In a jiffy she had them all under her umbrella, making sure they said exactly what she wanted; always passing the ball, always referring to her as 'Ma'am'. She's *grooming* these tenants for the media, Larry. They're ordinary folks; retirees, college kids, welfare mothers—people who've never in their lives imagined so much excitement, and who are all so conditioned, and so camera-shy, they'll say whatever she wants if it'll get them out of the spotlight. And once they've stammered themselves dry, there's this great, pregnant silence. The matriarch rises ominously from her extra-large folding steel throne, the sole focus of every lens. Then, speaking to the camera in measured tones, she tells all the rapt little housewives exactly what they want to hear: the Devil is stalking them; an invisible, irresistible, horny as all get-out satyr who's going to mesmerize them—remove their Christian guilt complexes, if you will—by *forcing* them to orgasm while their indifferent hubbies are off pursuing silicone secretaries. A sense of infidelity, just like in fantasy, becomes *okay* if you're not responsible. It's all very primal: poor helpless woman raped by nasty monster. And digs it! You know what I'm talking about, buddy? The 'victim's' sexual gratification justified. But where was maritally-celibate, totally inconsiderate husband when Evil Rapist was repeatedly doing oh-so innocent, frantically humping housewife? Who knows? Ask his bimbo secretary."

Abram had to break in. "Nelson, on most days I'd be more than happy to entertain a twisted philosophy based on a daily dose of assaultive scumbags and the women who love them, but—"

"*But*...back to our story: Dissatisfied housewives are descending *en masse* on the landlady's table, as giddy with the moment as she. Sex is in the air. Local ratings skyrocket. And believe me, it sure doesn't hurt that this Marilyn Purly is a total knockout. Yet the only *relevant* issue is some at-large pervert who's about to be lionized by a retentive society—turned into a romantic figure hunted by a world so uptight with its own sexual repression it's almost horny for a Judas goat."

"Remarry, Nelson, *remarry!* I must have told you a thousand times. You were never like this when you had an anchor."

"Larry, I'm putting it straight for you: there's a real danger of this jerk being turned into a kind of modern, persecuted Don Juan. They'll airbrush his booking photo—Oprah and her ilk will present him as the prey instead of the predator. And the 'You go, girl; you vent against that evil Mr. Rapist' mindset will quickly peter out. Why? Because the housewives aren't really mad at this sick prick. They're pissed at a very witting evil: the hubbies who somewhere along the line lost interest in them. They'll transfer. Just you watch. In an almost surreal way they'll get back at hubby and his hypothetical office bimbo by rooting for the rapist."

"Alleged rapist," Abram sighed. "Now look, Nelson, I'll concede Vilenov's no pretty boy, and I'll even admit the public's reaction is understandable, but there'll be a real backlash to all this dumping on some poor guy just because of his looks. You're right on one count, but for the wrong reason. What we've genuinely got here is a martyr in the making. When he's brought in, and the public gets a peek at the gentleman behind the image, he's not gonna be the heavy." He sipped thoughtfully, and found his drink oversweet. "And yes, there'll be lawsuits."

"Okay, buddy. You can address your flocks whenever you're ready. Right now, Vilenov's a fugitive, and that's all that matters. And when he's apprehended, Larry, I know you'll be right there on the tube with me, and you'll speak eloquently on his behalf. And a big part of me prays you're right—that the complaints of all these women are much ado about nothing. But if what I know in my heart is true, I'm gonna see this ugly SOB put away permanently. *Excuse* me, Larry, but was that chocolate milk and Newsweek your little angel picked up at Barry's on his way to Purly's? You go ahead and argue all you want about videotape and testimony to the contrary. But I'm gonna tell you something man-to-man here: your client stinks like shit warmed over. And if you really intend to represent him, you'd better make damned sure he saved all that cash he says his daddy left behind. He'll need it. Every cell in my body tells me he's going down, and for good."

"Okay, Nelson. Point made."

"So what's your move?"

"I'd like to interview Purly while her memories are fresh."

"They'll still be collecting samples."

"And there's that hold-out tenant."

"Frederick Mars, no middle. Upstairs in the twin building. Number 11."

Abram took it down in his notepad.

"You might also touch bases with Scarboro. But I'm warning you, right up front, to be extremely critical of anything you get from her."

"I'm always critical."

"I know you are, buddy. Thanks for the call-back. And let me know your read on that whole daffy setup."

Abram put down the receiver, killed what was left in the thermos, and switched on the TV. Vilenov's face leaped right out at him. Abram instantly muted the sound and pushed himself out of his chair. Halfway to the refrigerator he stopped, disturbed by the way Vilenov's projected eyes seemed to be following him across the room. He tiptoed to the wall plate and switched off the light.

Now the darkened room was lit only by the pallid face of Nicolas Vilenov with its floating gray eyes. The eyes followed him back to his chair, watched him recline, held him where he sat. A sudden psychotic loathing remade Abram's expression, cramped his fingers and toes and radiated throughout his body. For a moment he couldn't breathe or swallow. He wanted to smash something, kill somebody. His hand, flailing on the table, came back holding the slim remote unit. He raised it slowly and aimed it at the set. The eyes tugged at him, swelling in their sockets.

Abram hit the OFF button and the room plunged into utter darkness.

"Bang," he said.

Chapter Four

Mars

Despite the DA's warning, Abram was blown away by the circus on Westminster Avenue. He had to park a mile and a half down; the curb spot, payable up front to a hard-as-nails homeowner, cost him twenty bucks and an earful. Luckily a rookie traffic cop, recognizing him from his splendid performance in the final Jackson molestation case, gleefully transported him like a green chauffer delivering his first movie icon.

Ten a.m., and it was already cooking. Westminster was spilling over with blankets and tarps, with beach umbrellas and folding chairs. Catering trucks were pulled into the driveways of residences, in some places brazenly parked on sidewalks and lawns. The area's immigrant vendors, having cannily traded their oranges and flowers for garlic wreaths and rattan crucifixes, could sporadically be seen dashing through traffic like figures in a bull run. Curbside amateur artists sold soulful portraits of Vilenov the Christ-figure, Vilenov the snarling animal, Vilenov the rock star. The gushing officer drove Abram as close to Scarboro's apartment complex as the jostling crowd would allow. Abram then moved smiling and quipping through the slowly parting sea—past the reaching men and women shouting questions born of pure curiosity or outright fear, past the reporters and cameramen winging their booms and whirling their cams, past a fluid barricade of uniformed officers struggling to hold back the tide—all the way to the quiet drive between apartment buildings, where a single dour policeman stood within a broad rectangle of plastic yellow tape secured to rails and branches. **POLICE LINE**, the tape warned, **DO NOT CROSS**. The escorting officer begged shamelessly for an autograph, and the lawyer obliged. The rookie scampered off with his prize.

Abram turned to the residing officer with charm and humanity still smeared across his face. One look at the man's expression, and his smile collapsed. Abram automatically extended his attorney's hand in greeting. The uniform scowled and shook his head.

"You're over the line, Mr. Abram." He gestured at the lawyer's hovering arm. "In more ways than one."

Abram groaned. "Officer…"

"No way, Mr. Abram. This scene is being treated as a possible homicide."

Abram's sphincter clenched. "Homicide? Who…"

"Ah-ah-ah," said the uniform. "The star witness is *kaput*." He studied Abram coldly. "A tenant in this building," he jerked his head over his shoulder, "a Marilyn Purly, was discovered deceased in her apartment this morning after she was nonresponsive to a number of phone calls. She slit both wrists with a new razor blade. She knew how to do it, too. *Up* the vein, not across it." He demonstrated with an imaginary blade, watching Abram for signs of squeamishness. "She was found stone dead in her bedroom at seven hundred hours. The coroner says she did herself in around midnight. The black curtains in her bedroom were closed, the front room door was crudely wedged and blocked, and every light in the place was out except for the ring of bulbs on her vanity mirror. Oh, and one other thing. Before she goes for her wrists this hot young babe takes the razor and slashes her face into hamburger. The place looks like a slaughterhouse." He sucked the crud from his front teeth and respectfully spat to the attorney's side. "Now what do you make of that?"

But Abram's self-preservation instinct was screaming at him. Only a career built on poses allowed him to pull himself erect rather than shrink, and to reply in a voice that boomed with authority. He looked pointedly at the man's badge. "Officer Warren, your conduct couldn't be less professional. Who's your superior at this scene?"

The cop tossed his head at a sergeant just exiting Purly's unit. Drop cloths could be seen in front of the apartment and inside the doorway. "*Around* the tape!" Warren retorted, and watched minutely as the attorney navigated the narrow corridor defined by the building's staircase and taut police tape.

The sergeant ambled over after making a note on his pad.

"Good morning, sergeant," Abram offered congenially, his personal unease automatically moving to the back burner in the presence of authority. He wasn't remotely interested in reporting the surly cop; once circumvented, the man was history.

"Good morning, Mr. Abram. I'm sorry, but this perimeter is sealed for now."

"Gotcha. I'm really sorry to hear about Ms. Purly."

"I appreciate that, Mr. Abram. But the perimeter is sealed for right now."

Abram bowed, half-turning toward the mob. "Did I, sergeant, commend you on your security?"

"That, Mr. Abram, won't be necessary. And, forgive me, did I mention that this perimeter is sealed for now?"

Abram grinned and nodded. "Well, sir, I'd still like to interview a tenant or two, a Frederick Mars in particular."

The sergeant raised his eyes to the landing behind them. "That'll be fine, sir, but let's just make sure you stay clear of the police line." He jerked his head at the churlish guard. "And please confine your interviews to tenants."

Abram smiled and walked to the second floor landing's cement staircase. At the bottom of this staircase, squeezed between the building and trash dumpsters, a tiny laundry room poked out like a hemorrhaging tissue. Abram, facing the room's sole window as he stepped around the rail, experienced a brief, disturbing hallucination: hanging in the room's little window was an old navy blue beach towel. At some time a hose had dashed water across the glass, leaving it marked by a single spray of drops. To Lawrence Abram, just turning away from the sun, the immediate impression was a blood-spattered mirror. His hand slid up the iron rail as he casually climbed the steps, still looking back. For a nanosecond he thought the towel had been yanked aside to reveal the face of an extremely large, angry middle-aged woman. But the room's contents were hidden. There was no face.

On the upstairs landing to his left were five apartments. A single unit at the landing's end faced the staircase. Mr. Mars's door, like two others, was open, but Abram paused to lean deeply on the rail, so that his body nearly described a right angle. In this, the pose of a casual observer, he gazed across the drive into the open door of Purly's apartment.

It was an absolutely perfect view. *There* was the couch, and one corner of its large framed backing mirror. And *there*, directly across the room, was the old maple television cabinet, a black videocassette recorder planted firmly on top. The view was such that he could see a good part of the kitchen and most of the single doorway leading to bathroom and bedroom. The bedroom's black velvet curtains were down for analysis, sterile drop cloths carefully hung in their place. Occasionally an officer passed between rooms, into and out of Abram's view.

Feeling another presence, Abram turned and said pleasantly, "Mr. Mars?"

A lanky shadow appeared in 11's doorway. The sun lit a withered hand. "I'm Fred Mars."

Abram shook the hand, gently pulling the figure into full view. "Well, Mr. Mars," he said, his mind processing the snapshot: *black, seventy-something, frail, hint of Creole. Basically honest and forthcoming.* "My name's Lawrence Abram, and I've been retained to represent a certain Mr. Nicolas Vilenov, whose mismanaged arrest I pray is in no way related to today's most uncomfortable police presence. I didn't know Ms. Purly personally, but it breaks my heart to learn of her terrible passing. Were you a close friend of hers?"

"Miss Purly had lots of admirers," Mars said, "but she didn't have any friends. Except one. And this is the man you say you're representing. Perhaps he could help you more than me."

"Mr. Vilenov, alas, is presently unavailable. Um, you wouldn't have, by any chance, seen him around over the weekend? He's pretty easy to spot."

"No, sir, I most certainly would not have. And Miss Purly never once opened her door after that raid took place."

"About that arrest," Abram mulled. His arm swept the building and drive. "As I understand it, you had a pretty good eagle's eye-view of the event."

Fred Mars peered warily at the lawyer, then at the dawdling sergeant below. "Well...I..."

Abram reached into his vest's pocket. "Forgive me," he said, and handed Mars a business card.

Once he'd studied the card punctiliously, Mr. Mars placed it in his shirt's pocket with exaggerated care. His eyes slid down a rail to his visitor's black, highly polished calfskin shoes. "I'd invite you in, Mr. Abram, out of the heat, but I'm afraid I keep a very humble house."

Abram instinctively laid a hand on the man's shoulder. "Mr. Mars, you're embarrassing me. I'd be honored to be your guest, under any circumstances. Please realize you're doing me a favor just by talking to me—much more so by entertaining me. And I'd be delighted to share in whatever amenities you habitually make your own."

After an awkward moment Fred Mars apologized, almost in a whisper: "All I've got is beer. But it's cold; as cold as drinking beer can be. I pulled it from the freezer just this morning."

Abram's eyes slid away and his mouth turned down. "What—" he managed. "What *brand?*"

Fred Mars sank back. "Only Budweiser, I'm afraid."

"Thank *God!* Mr. Mars, I was afraid you were going to poison me with some of that sickly green imported stuff. But the King of American Beers! And icy cold, you say? I have a feeling this little interview isn't going to be so rough after all." He bowed toward the room. "Shall we?"

Mars, terribly embarrassed, creakily returned the bow. "Shall we, indeed."

Abram got comfortable on a small upholstered chair while Mars busied himself in the kitchen. The attorney's brain was a video camera: Pine coffee table. Yellowing magazines. Homey hunks of cheap furniture. A spotless ashtray. No more, no less than he was hoping for.

"Cold glass?" Mars fumbled from the kitchen. "Ice?"

"Not on a dare. It's already way too hot for manners between men. Let's get down, Mr. Mars, to brass tacks."

Fred Mars, smiling frailly, limped up with two ice-cold sixteen-ouncers. Abram saluted the room and gratefully downed a third, his eyes rolled back lovingly. Mr. Mars giggled and swallowed what he could, trying hard to look relaxed.

Abram wiped his lips with a forefinger. "Mr. Mars, I have exactly two things to say. The first is: thank you so much for helping me hit the spot. And the second is: God bless America!" He tilted back the can and chugged slowly, until there was only backwash, all the while studying his host from the corner of his eye.

Fred Mars was obviously unused to company. And craved it. He laughed softly while drinking, eyes closed and knees crossed awkwardly. Although Abram quickly killed his can fractionally, Mars managed to swallow over half as much by more frequently sneaking up on his own. Abram pinched his empty and raised an eyebrow.

Mr. Mars made a show of being above recycling. He tittered, determinedly killed his own beer and pinched the can, wobbled to his feet. He tossed both empties at a kitchen wastebasket, missed with one, picked it up and tried again, missed again. A neighbor on the landing laughed at the street mob. Blushing, Mars hurriedly trashed the can and looked outside.

Suddenly Abram felt California Good. It was just another make-believe day, perfectly hot and clear. A zephyr the moment it turned stuffy. Sunshine so clean an Angeleno could be myopic and still see wonders. *Real* sunshine. Beer weather.

"Mr. Mars," he said, "please feel free to call me Larry. And, if you'll honor me with another beer, I'll gladly repay you with an extra large pizza."

Fred Mars padded out with two more tall frosty Buds. "Thank you so very much, Larry, but you don't owe me a thing. I'm just glad to be enjoying your company on this beautiful summer day. And you, Larry, may call me Fred." He placed the cans on coasters and nodded politely. "I'm guessing you have something to ask me concerning...that day."

"Just a few simple questions, in strictest confidence, about your observations." He was dawdling with his beer, waiting for Mars to move along with his own. The old man took painfully slow, delicate sips. But the attorney knew Mars's age would work against him. Abram popped open his new can and took it easy. He already had a buzz on, and the gorgeous day almost demanded he drink deeply. His mouth was dry before the beer hit his stomach. And the brew was *so* cold. "By the way, Mr. Mars...Fred, what inspired you to call channel five?"

"It's my landlady, Miss Scarboro. Maybe you've run in-to her, Larry. If you haven't, I'm sure you soon will." He managed to down a quarter of his second can, as if just speaking her name left a bad taste in his mouth.

"I know about her."

"Well, she's a very pushy woman, Larry, a *very* pushy woman. She *pushed* everybody in these buildings into a tenants' committee, then she *pushed* everybody into believing Miss Pur-ly was being drugged and abused by some poor guy none of us had ever even met." After catching his breath he took another healthy swig. Abram immediately followed suit. "She just flat out didn't like this man, and told us he was an agent of Satan. She said she'd cast a spell to protect us, but that the only way to fight for poor Miss Purly was to band together, and use our combined energy to cast him out." His expression was hesitant, guilty.

Abram spread his hands. "I'm following you, Fred. And I'm not saying you bought into it. I know you've got more sense than that."

"I do *not* like being *pushed*. And I do *not* respect this Miss Scarboro person." Mr. Mars pulled at his beer. "Speak of the Devil!"

"So this tenants' committee," Abram fished, "was the force of Goodness, rallied against the force of Darkness? And anyone not adamantly pro-committee was..."

"Larry, I've been disgusted with Miss Scarboro from the get-go. She's a witch, but not in the supernatural sense. She's a witch wannabe. And she does dearly love to get people to an-swer to her...excuse me, Larry, to her...B.S."

"Go on, Fred."

"She hammered her ideas into our heads, and made sub-tle threats about possible evictions. It was all pure baloney. But as long as you fell in line the heat was off you, and she'd work on the next tenant. Mr. Abram, I don't know what she had a-gainst this fellow, but there was some real bad blood between them. I used to watch her shouting bloody murder through the space between the door and jamb. Miss Purly would refuse to take down the chain, and Miss Scarboro would stand hunched in front of that door like a fighting bull, her head down with that big straw hat half-covering her face, almost as if she was shield-ing her eyes. But Miss Purly always ended up closing the door on her, and Miss Scarboro always ended up stomping back to her apartment to cuss out the walls. It would have been really funny if it wasn't so intense. Then, once this gentleman was gone, Miss Scarboro would confront Miss Purly in a kinder mood, but Miss Purly would just zone out whenever Miss Scar-boro mentioned him directly. Otherwise Miss Purly seemed o-kay; okay enough to catch the bus to do her shopping, any-way." He raised an eyebrow. "Sir, I personally witnessed Miss Scarboro use her master key to go through that apartment a number of times when Miss Purly was gone."

"It's her building," said the attorney.

"And then she'd come out, gather us all in her little back yard over lemonade and cookies, and tell us over and over that Miss Purly was being drugged and raped by this stranger in some kind of horrible dark ritual. She got all the tenants focused into an unblinking rage. Everybody but me. I'll discuss any-thing with anybody, Mr. Abram, but nobody can *push* me. Pret-ty soon Miss Scarboro started on me with the silent treatment, then with the Evil Eye. And she passed around a petition, and got everybody but me to sign, stating that this guy was doping Miss Purly and having his way with her. She'd worked hard on the other tenants, until they believed her unconditionally. No-body understood why I couldn't deal with the 'truth'."

"Sounds like she'd make a great prosecutor."

"So Miss Scarboro sent copies of this petition to the police and to the news stations; radio and television. The police contacted Miss Purly by phone, and apparently an expert invest-igator listening in was convinced Miss Purly was under the influence of some pathogenic substance. I know all this because I received a letter from a Commander Burroughs, wondering why I was the sole committee holdout, and asking me if maybe

I'd be a witness if anything came down. I agreed, no problem, Mr. Abram, and I'm ready to be subpoenaed if that's what it takes."

Mars now became involved in a delicate little tap dance. Abram understood; his own bladder was floating. Being host, Mars switched on the old black and white TV. "I'll be right back," he grimaced, "Larry," and tiptoed into the bathroom.

Abram watched a televangelist passionately lecturing on rape as the natural consequence of a God-weary society. He leaned forward and turned the fat plastic knob a notch, from 4 to 5. A commercial appeared, featuring a line drawing of a horrified woman crouching beneath hovering eyes. Abram heard a voice urging Internet participation as a graphic leaped across the screen: *catcharapist.com.* He cranked the knob up to channel 7, but before the station came in he heard an eager recorded voice on 5 say, *"Rape survivors! Next on—"*

In a heartbeat he'd forgotten his bladder.

There was Nelson Prentis, at a podium surrounded by microphones. Behind the DA was a huge symbolic check for fifty thousand dollars. The letters WFW were emblazoned in the check's upper right hand corner.

Lawrence Abram grew excited every time his childhood friend appeared onscreen. He hunched forward with the can dangling between his fingers, mesmerized by those deadly-serious drooping eyes behind the black, severe spectacles, by the salt and pepper crew cut, by the wide and mirthless mouth, by that rich baritone that instantly filled a room. Who but Prentis's ex-wife and few close friends knew of the warmth and humor behind the efficient public image… "are banded today," Prentis was booming magnificently, "out of concern for the basic inviolability of our neighborhoods, for the security of our God-given sense of decency, and for the abiding safety of our sweet, priceless children. All our hearts are whelming over; as intelligent and sympathetic Angelenos we are deeply moved by the number of caring citizens who have come forward, with strong voice and with great generosity, to support the South Bay's branch of Women For Women." Prentis half-turned. "Today this check for fifty thousand dollars is being offered to any person or organization providing information leading to the apprehension of escapee Nicolas Vilenov!"

Behind him, Mars said quietly, "Not showing a picture, I notice."

Abram hadn't heard the flush. "Smart move. Enough is enough." He shook Mars's elbow and grinned up at him mistily. "I used to write for that man!" Mars smiled back as his guest rose and swaggered into the bathroom. When Abram returned he found the old man perched gingerly on the little padded chair, looking like he was about to be sucked into the big television's screen.

Channel 7 was now featuring the Westminster crowd in a live shot. As the videocam panned to a reporter in the mob's midst, the studio camera pulled back to reveal a poker-faced talking head at his desk. Thus superimposed, the bluescreened broadcaster matter-of-factly announced the reporter's name, location, and situation. The studio camera cut out, leaving the mobbed reporter to comment over a wide shot now zooming onto Marilyn Purly's open door. That shot was cut, and once again the screen was all street mob.

Fred Mars tiptoed outside and leaned half over the rail, obeying a childish impulse to be, even for an instant, on camera. Abram, listening to crowd members granted their fifteen seconds, was riveted. What amazed him was not so much the absurdity of the responses, but their complete sincerity. He told himself, over and over, *This is the 21st century. These are healthy, educated people.*

What proof have we, a grown man wondered, that Nicolas Vilenov's spirit didn't somehow infiltrate the premises to murder Ms. Purly? A man in a white shirt and tie assured him that the place was solidly monitored; a greased eel couldn't have slipped in. *But,* a soccer mom countered reasonably, how do we know Vilenov can't make himself invisible, or sneak through by morphing into a cop? This woman wore an extra large T-shirt with a silk screen image on either side. On the front was a glaring, terribly dignified portrait of the Scarboro woman surrounded by smoking censers. On the back was that cold, ubiquitous booking photo, smack in the middle of a circle containing a diagonal bar that cut the face into halves. A pimply UCLA student solved the problem for both parties. Ghosts, he explained, and sometimes even modern zombies, are capable of movements beyond the senses. But then a hypertensive genius behind the reporter began jumping up and down, holding a placard bearing an enlarged photocopy of Marilyn Purly's state I.D. "He's the Devil!" she screamed. *"The Devil!"* There was a roar of approval.

Abram and Mars listened as the roar tore up the drive like floodwater. The suddenly-erratic crowd image switched back to studio. 7's apologetic broadcaster, shuffling a handful of papers, described a series of clips unfolding on the screen behind him. The first showed a covered body; being wheeled from Purly's apartment, loaded into an ambulance. The landlady's face faded in as the ambulance faded out. Abram's eyes narrowed. *275 pounds,* he thought, *well over six feet. An absolutely formidable woman. Hostile witness. Will not answer an honest question honestly.* He unconsciously canceled his plans for an afternoon interview. Scarboro was replaced by a wide-angle shot of a typical suburban street. Dozens of children were lined up in ranks well away from the curbs. A woman on each sidewalk, wielding a STOP sign and pursing a nickel-plated whistle, preceded the files. These women methodically halted at houses, performed right faces and marched up to front doors. Grateful mothers handed over cringing schoolchildren. The orange-vested monitors then marched back with their precious cargo in tow. Flanking sidewalk monitors, stamping in strict time, guided the children to places in the rear rank. With a choreographed blast of whistles and jerk of STOP signs, the parade moved up to the next set of houses.

Imitating the voice of Mister Rogers, Fred Mars mumbled, "Can you say 'change of venue'?"

Abram said, "Come here a minute, Fred." Mars followed him out onto the landing. "Let's see where you were standing when those officers broke into Ms. Purly's apartment."

Mars took a few steps to his right.

"And how were you standing?"

The old man casually leaned on the rail.

"Excuse me, Fred." Abram slid into Mars's place while gently nudging him along. They stood shoulder-to-shoulder. Abram relaxed his knees, his forearms weighing on the rail. "Like this?"

"Exactly like that."

Abram was now standing a few feet to the right of his earlier vantage point. He looked into Purly's apartment. Couch and end tables were draped, but the huge backing mirror was still uncovered. And reflected in that mirror could be seen the innocently-perched videocassette recorder. Evidence tags were everywhere.

"When that whole scene came down, Fred," Abram said carefully, "what *exactly* did you see through Ms. Purly's front room doorway?"

"Larry…what I saw was the personal business of Miss Purly and her guest. I'm no voyeur. I only saw what I saw because it was downright unavoidable."

"But you saw…"

"I *saw*," Mars said with finality, "Miss Purly and her guest minding their own business. That's all, sir."

"Watching television. Sipping iced tea."

"Minding their own business."

Abram smiled at Mars's resolve. But suddenly he saw himself from the old man's unlettered viewpoint—as an arrogant authority figure; someone who would, five minutes after pretending to bond with you, aloofly spin your story for the sake of his case. Right on the tail of this little insight came the feeling that this viewpoint actually wasn't Mars's own. It hit him: Mars in truth wasn't the kindly observer he made himself out to be. Abram's wry grin twisted into a bitter snarl. Mars was an eyewitness and a rat, a pig and a liar. No way could he be allowed to testify. It became urgently important that Abram know *exactly* what Mars *had* seen. He placed a hand on the man's forearm, and heard a voice that was not really his, wheedling, "Oh, *sir*, I'm not prying, *believe* me I'm not. And I respect your right to not divulge a thing. But you've *got* to understand something here. *I'm* the one who's going to be defending this poor guy. I'm all the hope he's got."

Mars could have sworn he saw something burning in the attorney's eyes. He looked away. "I observed those policemen breaking in on Miss Purly and her caller. But I didn't see any tea. What I saw was a whole lot of skin." Abram bristled. A moment later he was himself again. "And I watched the police jump on Miss Purly's gentleman friend, and knock him around while he tried to get his pants on. I saw this one mean-looking policeman in plain clothes twist his arm behind his back and really rough him up while cussing in his ear—foul stuff, Mr. Abram, language I would never repeat. This went on while the policemen at the front door kept neighbors back, even as Miss Scarboro urged them on. An officer inside covered up poor Miss Purly, and had her spit in a plastic bag. He took her into the kitchen. The officer questioning Miss Purly came back out and said something to her visitor, then made a phone call while the man was forced to dress. Miss Purly's boyfriend was handcuffed and led outside, shoved through everybody and stuffed in a police car. And they weren't exactly gentle with him."

Abram grunted. An odd memory fragment came to him, crumbling even as he attempted to put his finger on it. Something in his subconscious warned him not to pursue the thought, but another part of his mind wasn't about to let it pass. "Fred, during any of this did you directly exchange glances with Mr. Vilenov?"

"No, Mr. Abram, I most certainly did not." A change came over Mars's voice, and Abram realized, without turning, that Mars was staring at him with great feeling. "By that time I'd seen more than I could stomach for a lifetime." Abram nodded. Figuratively standing in Mars's shoes, he visualized Vilenov at work. The urge to commit mayhem on the man seemed a perfectly rational and healthy reaction.

"Now you know how I felt," Mars mumbled.

There was a pause. Abram said, "If you really felt that way, why did you hold out on that petition?"

Mars took a deep breath. "Larry, I believe that what goes on behind closed doors is nobody's business but the parties concerned, so long as there's consent. If Miss Purly invites a man over, that's her affair. Miss Scarboro had no business interfering, and the police shouldn't have compromised their privacy. That said, I'm not bleeding for that dirty fellow they took in, regardless of how it may appear. The man's rights are my concern, not the man himself." There was a longer pause. At last Mars said, "So why are you really here, Larry?"

Abram shrugged. "I've been retained. I have a reputation to uphold, and I'm *going* to win this case."

"With *that* client?" Comprehension dawned on Mars's face. "You're here to have me subpoenaed, aren't you Larry?"

"With *that* testimony?" Abram shook his head. "But I want you to understand that you *will* be subpoenaed, Fred, though not from my side of the fence. You represent what will be the first real piece of evidence in this whole mess, and that's eyewitness testimony." He chucked Mars on the bicep. "Pretty soon, my friend, your name is going to be a household word. That crowd out there is going to become infected by Mars-mania. But don't worry. Even for a decent man celebrity has its compensations."

Mars looked sickened by the thought. "So. Where do we go from here?"

Abram drummed his fists on the rail. His mind was made up. "Fred, you bust us open a couple more cold ones and I'll make a phone call. Let's see if Domino's can get a pizza with the works through that crowd out there."

Chapter Five

Phelps

The old man and his young guide seemed to bob as they tramped up the crumbling asphalt walk, an apparent motion created by the old man's chronic limp working in conjunction with the boy's frequent missteps in sinkholes. It was very dark on the Venice Canals. Although freaked-out mallards occasionally hopped singly into bushes on the right, or plunged in manic clusters into the canal to their left, the neighborhood fowl colonies for the most part glumly tolerated the silently rocking figures. The boy was black, the old man a Finn, but in the dark they were devoid of race and nationality.

The boy tugged on the old man's finger. The old man looked down, his brown old brow furrowed under his blue old watch cap. The boy, nodding urgently, indicated an unimpressive cottage swallowed in a jungle of yard. The old man's eyes narrowed. No bars on the windows, no signs of real security. Only a sagging picket fence choking in weeds. On the rustic mailbox was hand-lettered the name *E. ROSE*. A painted American Beauty was positioned in the lower right-hand corner, like a signature.

The old man pulled a scruffy old handkerchief from his scruffy old trench coat. Wrapped in the handkerchief was a few dollars in pennies and nickels, bound at the top by a dirty old bit of string. The old man solemnly placed it in the boy's hand, closed the trembling little fingers over the bundle, and clasped the boy's hand in both of his. He shut his eyes and nodded, slowly and with gravity, before releasing the boy's hand. Rolling his eyes, the boy slunk off hugging his treasure to his chest, not daring to look back.

Ivan Phelps wistfully watched the dark figure vanish over a bridge. After a while he turned and looked the property up and down. Without seeming to move, he melted into the high weeds and trees. The limp was gone.

Phelps unlaced his boots and left them in the weeds with his socks. The old man walked barefoot on a path of inlaid bricks, taking long pauses between steps. When he reached the backyard he stopped dead. His eyes ran over the house, finally resting on the wide-open bathroom window.

Phelps removed his trench coat and placed it carefully on the ground. He was now wearing only his dirty old long johns. From under his left arm he gently extracted a filthy torn pillowcase containing an ancient baseball bat, a cheap plastic flashlight, a rusty pair of handcuffs, and a ratty length of rope. The rope, protruding from the pillowcase's open end, was wound tightly around the outside to prevent the contents from shifting. Phelps stepped very quietly to the window and peered into the bathroom. The house was absolutely dark. For a full minute he didn't move or breathe. He was feeling the place.

The old man raised the bundle above his head with the utmost slowness and, keeping it perfectly horizontal, carefully guided it through the window. He very gradually turned the bat clockwise, allowed it to dangle, then let the rope pass through his lax fist until the bundle just kissed the bathroom's tiled floor. He looped the rope's loose end about the window's hinge.

Ivan Phelps rested his forearms on the sill, testing its strength, and found it satisfactory. He filled his lungs. Throwing all his concentration into his arms and shoulders, he slowly ascended the outer wall like a great pallid lizard, using his toes for balance and coordination. It took a full five minutes for his waist to reach the sill, and by that time his face was purple and his head pounding. But Phelps's respiration was absolutely steady. He didn't make a sound. After only a few seconds' rest, he let his upper body ooze over the sill and into the dark bathroom. Whereas Phelps had used his bare toes as tender feelers on the way up, he now used his fingertips as sensitive probes on

the way down. Five more excruciating minutes, and he was ex-
amining the floor with his palms. Toe by toe, he walked his feet
down the inner wall until his body lay curled in a limp pool.

He did not get to his feet, but gripped each end of the
bundle squarely and fully extended his arms. Gently pushing off
with his toes, he crossed the floor like a snake. Five silent minutes later he was poised in the bathroom doorway. Holding the
bat absolutely horizontal while balancing his entire weight on
his sternum, Phelps rolled his bulging eyes left and right. His
ribcage felt like it would collapse at any moment, but he would
not let the probe dip a centimeter. There was too much at stake.
And besides, the old man knew all about pain.

Directly ahead was the living room. To the left, a short
hallway and kitchen. Phelps was reading an accurate mental
snapshot of the cottage's interior, produced solely from his outside inspection. The only bedroom lay to his right. The snake
made a very slow right turn and patiently slithered, all thighs
and pectorals, to the open bedroom doorway.

Phelps spent much longer here, letting his eyes adjust to
the room. The shades were down; nothing other than the bulk-
iest objects were discernible. But he smelled prey. Phelps let his
own breathing fall in with the naked woman snoring gently beside the obscure man on the bed. When their rhythms were one
he became aggressive, ever so slowly ratcheting up the woman's snores until their compound sawing took subconscious
hold of the sleeping man. In just under half an hour all three
were practically howling in perfect sync. Phelps began worming
across the carpet, sweat falling off his face like bombs. Twenty
minutes later he was on his knees beside the bed, still snarking
away like crazy. He delicately unraveled the bundle. With his
eyes closed, he laid out his tools one by one.

Phelps now became a hunched statue; the pillowcase
dangling from his left hand, the bat gripped in his right. The
long plastic flashlight was clamped in his teeth, its lens directed
at the black figure almost under his nose. Inch by inch, he raised
his left hand until its index finger lay poised on the flashlight's
power switch.

Phelps spent less than a second verifying the sleeping
man's identity. He switched the flashlight on and off, carefully

removed it from his mouth, set it between his knees. Guided only by that brief look, he yanked the pillowcase over Vilenov's
head and brought the bat down with all his force.

The woman sat up screaming bloody murder. Ignoring
her, Phelps pulled the rope tight around Vilenov's neck and savagely knotted it at the back. He flipped his limp prisoner over
and slapped on the cuffs, all the while speaking patiently to the
woman shrieking almost in his lap.

"Ye'll be hollerin a whole lot less, ma'am, an ye'll be
thankin me, ye will, soon as ye learn what I'm doin is fer yer
own sake." He hauled Vilenov onto the floor with a crash. "I do
apologize, ma'am, I surely do. But this is one fish what won't
be gettin away." Phelps knelt, grabbed Vilenov by a wrist and
ankle and threw him over his shoulder. "Kindly jus set yerself
back down to sleep now, ma'am. Yer worries are over."

Phelps's capture of The Houdini-rapist made him an instant celebrity. He used the reward to buy the inboard of his
dreams, made a few more bucks in a whirlwind of awkward talk
show appearances, and vanished from the harbor late one lovely
summer evening. He was never heard from again.

The public's attention soon shifted from Helga Scarboro's obscene struttings to the fascinating riddle of Nicolas Vilenov. But the eagerly anticipated smutty confession was not
forthcoming: Phelps had walloped him so hard he could barely
mumble. The first few days were a nightmare of tests and interviews, of clamoring reporters and six o'clock feedings. Nelson
Prentis rose to the occasion with both humor and sobriety, providing the barking press liberal tosses of quality sound bites—
all to the effect that Nicolas Vilenov, a physically-and mentally
incapacitated prisoner, would remain a prisoner.

Much was made of Vilenov's cracked skull.

Those believing his escape was achieved through some
weird paranormal ability warned that Phelps's blow might have
only phased him. Opposing this view, a rational faction voiced
profound sympathy for Vilenov as scapegoat and victim of the

system. Members of the former camp were labeled "Hysterics" by the latter. The Hysterics, in turn, labeled their detractors "Enablers." A running shouting match grew uglier by the day.

Nicolas Vilenov was maintained in special confinement at Western State Hospital, where brain specialists confirmed what was apparent to all: temporal lobe damage had left him weak as a kitten. His manacles were removed. Everyone agreed that Vilenov, shattered and under continuous observation, would not be pulling off his now-famous vanishing act any time soon.

There were basic and exclusive tests. Blood and urine, EKG, ECG, neuro-monitoring stress-and-sleep. Vilenov was shocked and graphed, sampled and scoped, pricked, scraped, tapped and palpated. They picked his mind until he wanted to scream. It was all filmed and digitally saved, extensively analyzed and exhaustively reviewed. Results were always in the normal range. But the tests were kept coming, if only to mollify the public during those furious first days. On the third day, when many Hysterics were peaking, a wooden Nicolas Vilenov was wheeled outside for a news conference, a heavy bandage wound round his head. His mouth gaped, his chin grazed his chest in a permanent nod. And, most important, his eyes were glazed and distant, unable to focus on any proffered object. It was a pathetic appearance.

But it turned the tide for Vilenov-watchers, and made Hysterics look like a bunch of pitiless bashers. The moment those soulless cameras lingered on that broken gaze, the public's initially ambivalent outcry became a howling plea to spare man from man. Umbrageous Enablers took center stage, while Hysterics could only peep from the wings with half-baked charges of a state-orchestrated appearance by a Vilenov look-alike.

The Enablers (a tag they hated at least as much as the Hysterics hated theirs) took to the streets exhorting individual civil rights, and overnight mustered an Internet mob that swarmed the medical center for a 24/7 candlelight vigil. Like all well-meaning liberals, Enablers clung to the ideal of a generic decent American whose Constitutional rights were even more important than the system that had bled profusely for those rights. It didn't matter that Vilenov was a particularly nasty customer without national identity, accused of being an all-around predator and serial rapist. He was, to Enablers, the presumed-innocent victim of a society still in denial of its hoods and sheets.

But Hysterics, buttressed by a surprisingly robust and vocal Moral Majority, utilized every opportunity to pose brave-ly with cowering wives and children, verbally smiting Enablers and Don't Knows alike, until both siding with Vilenov and in-difference were synonymous with Satan worship. This self-feeding passion was described by the governor, famously, as "that silly downstate wildfire," and soon L.A.'s much-publi-cized excesses were being eagerly blamed for the entire Vilenov affair. The rest of the nation looked on, first with a corn-fed, purple-mountains curiosity, then with that Very East Coast der-ision known as *California Envy*.

Disgust descended like God on the troubled South Bay.

As rumors of Vilenov's alleged trespasses surfaced, news stations jumped on the bandwagon, interviewing anybody with a grievance and a suntan. Nationally, eyewitnesses to Vi-lenov rapes and molestations popped up in places Vilenov had manifestly never heard of. A *hunger* sounded in the nation's up-right, well-manicured streets. Even in the Bible Belt, rape be-came *sexy*. Soap operas, talk shows, supermarket tabloids would dwell on nothing else. Nicolas Vilenov, or at least his two-dimensional specter, simply would not go away.

Although it's the practice in L.A. county to file a case in the judicial district where the crime occurred (which in this instance was Santa Monica), the DA filed the case downtown, away from the carnival-like energy of the Venice Beach com-munity. Vilenov was arraigned in absentia, far too ill to make an appearance. On the strength of semen data and crime scene sig-natures, Nicolas Vilenov was charged with multiple counts of rape and forced entry. His trial date was arranged to coincide with his doctors' go-ahead, and his bail set in the ionosphere.

In Abram's and a trustee's presence, a groggy Vilenov angrily waived his right to a jury trial. He cursed all of Abram's personalized defense strategies, instructing him to instead im-press the court with lurid details of the Vilenov philosophy. The attorney was ordered to not pursue change of venue, and to insist courtroom cameras be prohibited. Also, he demanded the removal of a specific psychiatrist, one Doctor Edward Reis, who he claimed was in the practice of ridiculing him, and harassing him with bizarre and unorthodox procedures, most notably conducting sessions in the dark. He then gave the lawyer the combination to a second storage locker, and told him to "get busy."

Within that locker, in large bills stuffed in a fat canvas bag, Abram found a considerable fortune. His previously narrow eyes grew wide in his head. He began visiting this shrine on a daily basis.

Lawrence Abram hired assistants, conferred with specialists, and interviewed dozens of prospective witnesses—but everything he turned up only made him loathe his client more. The Purly sample matched semen taken from the homes of seventy-four hysterical women. There were scalp and pubic hairs, clothing fibers, fingerprints almost too numerous to catalogue. A dead man would have been aware of Vilenov's guilt. And there were the inadmissible but very damning videotape, the claimant location photos, and that signed affidavit from the Purly crime scene. Ordinarily this affidavit, attesting to the validity of the sample obtained, retained, and deposited by Ms. Purly, would have been tantamount to eyewitness evidence, for it was signed by Purly, the scene's senior officer, and the forensic man responsible for its transport to Parker Center. But Abram understood that lack of remembrance on the part of surviving signatories would render the document worthless; it could not be recognized under oath. Just so: every speck of physical evidence that could not be corroborated by testimony served only to prejudice the prosecution. And all these DNA-matched semen samples, now cropping up around the county, were next to useless so long as complicity between Vilenov and his "girlfriends" could not be ruled out. Irreducible testimony is concrete. Partial memories, misgivings, a sense of violation, mean nothing. Furthermore, tons of complaints came from women claiming violations *years prior* to the arrest. Why were these women silent so long? Were they really, as Prentis suggested, a flock of menopausal gadabouts crying wolf only because they were so desperate for attention? Lawrence Abram hired the best polygraphists in the state. It was easy as pie, using a lie detector, to dismantle the most complex statements with simple questions. Abram knew these women were dealing with *feelings*, rather than genuine recollection. And the audaciousness of some of their claims only served to undermine the believability of others.

Abram grew nervous and remote as Vilenov's physical condition improved, complaining of stomach aches and lancing pains. He actually seemed to shrink in stature when near his client. The knob on Vilenov's temple was now only a slightly discolored lump, yet he was plagued by crunching headaches, blackouts, and lapses in memory. The entire ward was affected by malaise during Vilenov's stay, and by deep depression following his occasional grand mals. Vilenov's hold on medical personnel was weak, but it was enough to change a few minds and bend opinions in his favor. He told Abram that his doctors were quite satisfied with his condition, and that a clean bill of health was already being prepared for submission to the court. Vilenov smiled wanly. The doctors, he said, were proud of him. When Abram tried to coach him for what would turn out to be the shortest criminal trial in L.A.'s history, Vilenov told him not to worry. The point was to get the trial over ASAP. All Abram needed to do was lend his presence and his legal acumen. Vilenov would do the rest. But Abram, still the strong partner in their relationship due to his client's injury, explained repeatedly, and occasionally with attitude, that the system was not a forum for egotistical sermons—that he, Vilenov, was not a very popular guy right now, and that there were a whole lot of things to worry about besides the trial. Such as the ongoing frenzy right outside, where a pair of Hysterics had recently kicked to death a lone Enabler and posed triumphantly while being taken into custody. Their shouted on-camera desire to share a cell with Nicolas Vilenov had created two awkward new heroes on one side and an unbidden martyr on the other.

When Vilenov was finally brought to trial in an L.A. courtroom, he arrived in a secure van followed by an endless parade of police cars, news vehicles, and groupie-like spectators.

Enablers felt the exclusion of cameras, lack of venue

change, sky-high bail, and non-jury trial demonstrated just how much control the state exerted over their precious symbol of persecution. That this setup was Vilenov's own wish, publicly supported by his famous attorney, meant less than nothing to the line of Enablers now running alongside the slow caravan, for in the context of their ideology it only revealed how incapable he was of taking part in his defense. They shouted rhyming slogans about the squelching of freedoms, based mostly on the fact that the media were (wisely) denied in-house interviews due to his "injuries and incoherence."

This first line of Enablers fumed as they ran. Alongside and behind trotted a motley mob, waving American flags of all sizes. Among these flags could be seen placards citing Jefferson, Franklin, and Adams, with an occasional Lincoln silhouette thrown in. On the mob's fringe were the megaphone toters, wearing Vilenov T-shirts and exhorting passersby to "stand for the man." Most arresting of the Enablers' gimmickry was a magnificent fifty foot-wide American flag, passed along like an Olympic Torch by a broken line of wheezing high school faculty volunteers.

On the convoy's other side Hysterics ran hooting, shaking their fists and shouting obscenities. Every other member carried a hot-selling placard featuring Vilenov's mug shot, the image cleverly made up with horns, fangs, and mangy goatee. Just behind were the chanting waitresses and swooning schoolmarms, the Ivan Phelps wannabes, and a miscellany of schoolboys, ruffians, and pickpockets. Then came a row of placards citing the Apostles, bobbing above a wide current of banding-and-disbanding groups. Finally, making up the fringe, were the so-called "Milk Carton Mothers," a subdued group bearing placards featuring enlarged photos of missing children and pets, famous murderers and runaway daughters. On the fringe of the fringe were the nuts and the noisemakers, the petty dope dealers and the darting soda vendors.

Through this miserable sea the police van and its entourage moved like the children of Israel. As the vehicles neared the courthouse a phalanx of riot police commenced a flanking maneuver. The train crept between parallel lines of manpower until the van reached the courthouse's very steps. The cargo door slid open, and a heavily-shackled Nicolas Vilenov was helped out by two men in suits. Vilenov, wearing a blind man's shades outfitted with crown-and chin straps, dropped his head in pain. After a moment of absolute silence a roar went up from the crowd. Vilenov doubled over. There were many elements constituting that mass ejaculation, but, depending on which direction you were leaning, it could have been described as either *soulless ecstasy* or *mindless outrage*.

The two men hustled Vilenov up steps flanked by cops in riot gear. On both sides of the staircase reporters popped up like jacks in the box.

Inside the building a mousy little man appeared and dramatically thrust outward the tall glass doors. The two officers pushed Vilenov up and through while the flanking cops closed behind him, forming a tight living wall.

The mousy man ran his eyes back and forth over the passion and pain. After a minute he sneered and pulled the tall doors shut with a slam.

Chapter Six

Hatch

Sandwiched between marshals, Vilenov was squeezed through the doors, bullied past the metal detector, and hauled down a long hallway stuffed to the gills with officers of the court, with private and municipal security, with countless newspersons thrusting cameras and microphones every which way. A narrow corridor bisected the crowd. Vilenov's progress was peristaltic, his body bruised up and down by the very officers assigned to protect him. Heads of the curious popped in and out of the corridor as he approached, popped in and out as he passed. He walked with a limp and a wince, the injured temple protected by his raised shoulder.

One of six assigned bailiffs held open the courtroom's doors. Three men in suits backed off spectators. Vilenov was stuffed into a brightly lit arena no less congested than the hallway. There were no camera stations up front; his bleak scaffold contained only the judge's bench and the witness stand, the attorneys' tables, a pair of high easels with blank boards, a folding table bearing computer and monitors, and an openly curious stenographer. A bailiff taped up two pre-measured cardboard squares, blocking those eager faces pressing the glass. He stood with his back against the doors, his hands clasped behind him. Lawrence Abram helped escort his client through the gate, but when he took his elbow Vilenov immediately yanked it away. "Touch me again and I'll bite your nose off."

"This is the point," Abram whispered, "where we drop all that." Only the black shades made it possible to view Vilenov directly. "If you want to be treated like a grown man you'll have to behave like one."

"Forgive me, counsel, but now is not a real good time to exercise your famous rhetorical bullshit."

"Then fire me! You're entitled to be your own defense. Free me and let me go back to the real world. Let me out of this nightmare."

"Not a chance, motherfucker. Not after all the cash you've glommed from me. You're gonna start earning it, *right now!*" This little outburst was torture to his temple. Vilenov lowered and wagged his head. In a minute he said quietly, "I'll have my say down the line, don't you worry, but it'll be *after* you've done your job. If you get me out of this jam I might be willing to let bygones be bygones. But if you don't…God help you." He slumped into a folding chair.

The prosecution's table seated two men and a woman, their minds apparently elsewhere. Icy lead prosecutor Baker was flanked by Manwell and Simms, both dead-serious deputy district attorneys. But right now all were rocking in their chairs and joking, infected by the hubbub. Vilenov jangled his chains and the rocking ceased. Three cold faces turned as one.

"Abram!" Sweat was seeping from Vilenov's sideburns. "I want these shades off!"

"You'll have to wait. I'll need to address his honor."

"Then address him well." He leaned back his hammering head. The pain was slow in passing, and when at last he heard a bailiff order everyone to rise he was too far gone to comply.

Abram looked down. "I suggest you not irritate the court, Mr. Vilenov. Insolence never plays well."

Vilenov carefully rolled his head and stared out of one eye. He had to admit that Abram cut an impressive figure. The man's expression was at once serious, amicable, studious, and game. Immaculately tailored and groomed, scrubbed almost pink. "The court, Mr. Abram," Vilenov said weakly, "will just have to deal with it."

Orin Hatch, glancing coolly at the defense table, moved

briskly to the bench, scooping scattered notes into a corner pile as he went. Vilenov sat upright, growling like a prodded animal. He quickly sized the passing man, the overhead fluorescents painting long swiveling white embers on his black glasses: early sixties, bespectacled, ruddy. Way overweight, wearing his jet robes like a muumuu. Thin white hair, military cut. *Okay, dickhead*, thought Vilenov. *Come on. Talk to me.*

Hatch seated himself with genuine command and deliberation, looking over the spectators as if they were children in an auditorium.

"Be seated," said the bench bailiff.

Hatch tapped a few keys on his laptop. "In the matter of Nicolas Vilenov," he said, looking at the screen, "this proceeding will move forthrightly and with dignity. The bench will not tolerate outbursts from the audience." He peered over his spectacles. "This is the only warning you will receive. I frankly do not appreciate circuses, and deeply respect the solemnity of a courtroom. Any courtroom. So please observe this admonition. Sit quietly and respectfully."

Vilenov rattled his chains.

The judge's head jerked a notch, as though he'd just dealt with a crick. His voice, deadly-quiet, still penetrated the room's every hollow. "*Anyone* frustrating this proceeding will be ordered removed."

Abram rose immediately. "Your honor, my client has expressed an urgent desire to be relieved of his very dark sunglasses, so that he may observe with clarity the state's evidence. He is completely restricted in his movements by what I can only describe as a superabundance of physical restraints. I see no reason he should also be visually impaired."

"He can't see what's going on around him?"

"These are the same dark glasses the blind employ, your honor. They are not designed for observation."

Hatch gestured impatiently with his fingers. A bailiff unsnapped the harness, peeled off Vilenov's shades, and handed them up. Hatch lifted the lenses and peered through. When he tilted the device for comparison's sake he found himself looking directly into the pale gray pools of Vilenov's eyes.

Hatch couldn't shake the stare. For a long time he appeared to be deliberating. Finally he said, "The court finds no reason for the defendant to be thus encumbered." He handed the dark glasses back to the bailiff.

Simms rose with an objection, but a hard look from the prisoner sat him right back down. Vilenov then turned slowly in his chair, his eyes drawing every face. The spectators' expressions quickly became slack, their eyes dull. Following the sweep of his gaze, their heads began to wobble like the heads of floating corpses. When Vilenov turned back, his chin was on his chest and his temple was throbbing. He squeezed shut his eyes and let himself drift, subconsciously aware of a long, monotonous procession of court proceedings, of technical jargon flying about amidst sputtering keystrokes and tramping feet. He must have dozed. When he raised his head again, Vincent Beasely was being escorted from the stand. Something far profounder than straightforward hatred contorted Beasely's expression as he was led by. His eyes were bugged and raving, his lips writhing, the muscles of his jaw working overtime. His face came at Vilenov like a snake. Vilenov, so startled he didn't have a chance to lock eyes, could only snap back his head. Knowing and sharing Beasely's abhorrence, the escorting officer nevertheless restrained him with a quick bending-back of the thumb. It was done with great professionalism. Clenching his teeth all the way, Beasely was thrust up the aisle and out the broad double doors.

"Your honor," Abram offered in the disturbance's wake, "officer Beasely's testimony concerning the raid at Ms. Purly's residence contrasts dramatically with the memories of his fellow crime scene officers. Without going so far as to color his sworn statement perjurious, I *will* say that it mirrors *only* the testimony of the state's surveillance specialists positioned in the apartment above. It seems pretty obvious that Beasely's present recollection is inspired by a viewing of this bizarre tape at some time subsequent to my client's arrest. As this tape is fundamentally inadmissible, I would move that Beasely's testimony also be ruled inadmissible."

Vilenov exchanged glances with the judge. Hatch squirmed a bit, squinched his head into his shoulders, and said testily, "So ruled."

From then on Vilenov's impressions were increasingly fleeting and disjointed. He would sink into the brief bliss of a-byss, only to be jolted by a phrase or name of particular significance. A few minutes of droning testimony, followed by a dream of cool, uncrowded places. Time lost all meaning for Vilenov. The parade of witnesses became a gently pulsing blur. Examination and cross-examination were oscillating murmurs. Judge Hatch's voice, gradually bringing it all to a focus, just as gradually let it all trail away. To Vilenov's tender senses, a verbal respiration permeated the room: voices swirled around him, sucked at him, bored through his eardrums, collided in his brain. He passed out. When he reopened his eyes his cheeks were wet with tears.

The scene had changed: Abram and Manwell were posed confrontationally between the easels and monitors.

One easel featured a blown-up photo of a legal affidavit bearing type and three signatures, the bottommost signature sprawled awkwardly across the page's lower half. The other easel supported an enlarged photo of the surveillance equipment used in monitoring Purly's apartment. Both monitors were active. One showed a graph with spiking lines, the other a broad field of brightly colored spectrographic readings.

The air was heavy as water. Manwell, her face drawn, stood clamping the folding table's edge with quivering hands. Abram, appearing focused and relaxed, had just turned to speak directly to the audience. The words made no sense to logy Vilenov: "...his polygraphed inability to corroborate the affidavit's signing is so glaring I would move that the affidavit itself be removed as evidence." He vaguely heard Hatch speak the name 'Carre' twice, then heard Abram respond emphatically, "*Again*, your honor, Carre's and Beloe's polygraph examinations *manifestly* prevent their swearing under oath. They *do not recall* providing signatures."

Something made Vilenov focus all his will on the prosecution's table. The judge looked at Baker, who dully shook his head.

"The evidence," Hatch said, "is so stricken."

A brief pang passed quietly. Vilenov managed a smile. All he had to do was stare and concentrate, then just kick back and watch the puppets dance. Abram was performing splendidly; his painted eyes and hinged jaw going through the motions without a hitch, his cufflinks and rings winking arrestingly. Although the prosecution was dead in the water and barely able to converse, Baker pushed himself to his feet. "Your honor, the state would like to call Dr. Bertrand Griffith to the stand. Dr. Griffith is a professor of biology at the University of Southern California. He is also a serologist in the occasional employ of LAPD, working out of Parker Center, and an expert in DNA evidence."

Hatch, catching himself drifting, jerked up his head and typed in Griffith's name. Vilenov watched intently as frail old Dr. Griffith, flustered by all the hallway activity, was ushered down the aisle and sworn in. Hatch highlighted the man's bio, responding to Griffith's spoken credentials with a succession of weary nods.

"Dr. Griffith," Baker began, looking down at his notes, "would you please tell the court the results of your DNA comparison tests on those semen samples taken from the residences of Marilyn Purly, Elizabeth Rose, and..." he completed the list of eleven names. "Can these samples be established as having a common source?"

Griffith creaked forward. His voice, even amplified, was as distant as the wind. "All aforesaid samples are undoubtedly from the same source."

"And, Doctor, isn't it true that the semen sample procured at the Purly residence was in fact a mixture of this common source semen with saliva demonstrated to be that of Marilyn Purly herself? Speak up, please."

Vilenov's eyes narrowed. He looked hard at his attorney.

Abram jumped up, shaking his head like a dog out of water. "Your honor, the testimony of this witness can only lead us all up a blind alley. The affidavit for that sample has been stricken. By extension the sample itself has no evidentiary value in this proceeding."

"Mr. Abram." Hatch paused as Vilenov's eyes pulled at him. With an effort he looked away, found himself, and continued. "A certain sample was tagged and transported to Parker

Center, where it was analyzed in conjunction with samples data from the sites of eleven other complainants. The technicians at Parker, as you are aware, are highly competent and thorough in their investigations. The equipment is state of the art." He rolled his laptop's mouse and tapped a few keys, calling up the Parker documents. "The court has access to all necessary data for these samples. Now, despite this remarkable gap in the memories of certain individuals at the actual arrest scene, it is quite possible to follow the trail of transporting signatures in reverse, from the lab back to the Purly residence, and to conclude that the sample in question did indeed originate there, without having to incorporate the stricken affidavit. The sample tag was not only signed, it was dated and clocked. Even the odometer readings have been tabulated, and illustrate that a train of transport leading to Purly's would be consistent within a tenth of a mile. It doesn't require a Holmesian leap to deduce that the stated sample is germane to both Ms. Purly and to the scene. Signatures or no. The sample will remain in evidence. Mr. Baker?"

"Thank you, your honor. Dr. Griffith, did the sample in question consist of common source semen mixed with saliva from the late Ms. Purly?"

Vilenov rattled his chains.

Griffith went absolutely pale. Hatch had to twice order him to sip water and clear his throat before the man was able to whisper timidly, "It did."

"And, Doctor, with all this confusion concerning signatures, conflicting statements, and unreliable eyewitness testimony, how are you able to ascertain that the crime scene saliva is actually Marilyn Purly's?"

Vilenov thrashed in his seat, sparks leaping in his pale gray irises.

Griffith looked like a man having a heart attack. "Purly," he gasped into the microphone, "provided detectives a saliva sample prior to the raid on her apartment."

"So you're telling the court that the mixture was obtained with foresight; that Purly herself was prepared to acquire an exhibit for the state in this manner?"

"Yes!"

Directly on that blurted word, the table holding computer and monitors collapsed with a double crash that jolted everyone in the room. One monitor rolled halfway across the floor to the gate bailiff's shoes. Dead silence. Two seconds later the audience erupted with shouts and uncertain laughter. Hatch immediately slammed down his gavel. While the bailiffs and stenographer set the table back up, he ordered a special officer brought in, then summoned both counsel to the bench. The new officer walked directly across the room and stood behind Vilenov. He rested his hands close together on the chair's back, his fingers just grazing Vilenov's shoulder blades.

A man of immeasurable ego, Vilenov had deluded himself, from the moment of his arrest to the very conclusion of Griffith's testimony, that Purly had in fact been set up, that she was his loyal girlfriend to the bloody end. But the doctor's sworn word was unassailable evidence of her betrayal; it was the final kick to a beaten man's pride. He closed his knees and arms, embracing himself pathetically. Vilenov shut his eyes so hard tears squeezed between the lids. Half a minute later he sagged.

The whisper in his hair snapped his eyes right back open.

"Good morning, sir. And how are you feeling on this lovely day? No, don't turn around. I've just been assigned to look after you—to make sure, for example, that nobody accidentally puts his hands around your throat and squeezes and squeezes until those ugly eyes of yours pop clean out of your head."

Vilenov sat perfectly upright.

"So it's important," the voice went on, "for you to be just as nice as you can possibly be. It's important because you're a very unpopular boy. As a matter of fact, you're so unpopular there isn't a man in law enforcement who wouldn't gladly give his eyes for the opportunity to rip your heart out." The voice sucked air with a serpentine hiss. "Do you know what a dead pool is, fuckface? A dead pool is a kind of game where friends bet to see which celebrity dies first, and the players get points depending on how old the dead celebrity is, calculating backward from a hundred. Well, we've set up our own little pool. The difference is there's only one celebrity, and the bet is how long you last from the time I lead your doomed ass out that door."

Vilenov's eyes urgently sought the bench, but Hatch was totally caught up with Abram and Baker.

"What I need to know up front," the judge was saying, "is just how dependent on that computer you two are. I've got no qualms about the system's viability—computers may crash, but they seldom burn. However, it's arguably a crippled situation. By the time a new system is brought in and verified as up-and-running we can all be well along if we focus on computer-extraneous material."

Baker said, "Under the circumstances, I think I've completed my examination of this witness. The prosecution's future need for technical support of testimony will exist only when the defense brings into play any technical questions concerning testimony."

"Fair enough," Abram said wryly, "and truly a mouthful." Tarantulas tugged at the hairs on his nape. Suddenly Abram was sweating profusely. "I'm not prepared to…" he stammered, "cross! I'd like…please—a quick word with my client."

Hatch nodded, an eyebrow arching. He and Baker watched curiously as Abram walked over to Vilenov, pausing halfway to glare at the restraining officer. The man, stolidly returning the look, stepped very stiffly to the gate and stood with legs wide and hands clasped behind his back, staring at the far wall. Hatch fiddled with his computer while Abram and Vilenov sank into a whispering huddle. Abram tore himself away and stepped back to the bench.

"Your honor, my client has voiced a real concern for his safety regarding the officer you've assigned. I would ask the court that this man be removed. Mr. Vilenov is more than adequately restrained, and poses no threat to the court or himself."

"Mr. Abram," Hatch said levelly, "the officer is necessitated due to your client's continued hostility to this proceeding. Since I'm certain you've had ample opportunity to instruct him on courtroom etiquette, I can only assume his behavior is beyond your control. I'm *not* going to allow him to manipulate. No more rattling of chains, no more conspicuous fidgeting. No more slumping or leering, no more moaning and groaning. As to the imposition of officer Welle, a thirty-year veteran and trusted personal friend; he is here solely to maintain order. Certainly his manner may seem gruff. He has a job to do; he's not here to spread a little sunshine. Furthermore, his very presence assures your client's safety, rather than compromises it." He drummed his fingertips impatiently. "I don't want to go into contempt here. Does counsel require extra time to refresh Mr. Vilenov on proper courtroom comportment?"

"No, your honor."

"Then we'll proceed."

Abram returned to his seat. The officer stepped back behind Vilenov's chair.

"Dr. Griffith, you may step down. Thank you for your contribution. Mr. Baker?"

"Your honor, I would like to call to the stand as state's witness Dr. Edward Karl Reis."

At the name Vilenov rose like a sidewinder. A pair of very strong hands put him straight back down.

Abram pressed his palm on Vilenov's forearm. With his mouth right up against his client's ear, he hissed, "Like it or not, you're going to have to control yourself! Maybe you didn't notice, but I just got chewed out thanks to your misbehavior. I've told you a thousand times that the worst thing you can do is get on the judge's bad side. He's a human being like anyone else."

"*That's* the one. *That's* the son of a bitch who tormented me in every session."

Abram shrugged angrily. Vilenov's attitude in full view of the court brought out a snarl of resentment. "Who? *Reis?* I don't give a damn if he's the Devil in drag. And guess what, pal: you're not exactly Mr. Warm-and-Fuzzy yourself. So just shut up already, and pretend you weren't born in a storm drain. Okay? Is that too abstruse for you? You're really screwing me here, and that only redounds to your disfavor. Besides, this isn't a contest. The man's here to testify."

Vilenov's mouth fell open. His eyes bulged in their sockets. "It is *too* a contest! And you *will* tell the judge you want his testimony barred! *Now!* The prick's a liar."

Abram jerked his face away. "I can't *do* that! I'm not running this show. Besides, I'd not only be out of order, I'd be out of my mind. So would you *please* just wait for him to complete his testimony? We'll have our chance."

"Get up, you thieving puppet," Vilenov whispered nastily. "*Up*, backstabber! Get...*up!*"

Abram peered at the bench.

Hatch was looking daggers. "What did we just discuss?" He thrust forward a hand, the thumb and forefinger spread an inch. "Counsel, you are *this* close."

Staring coldly at Abram, Baker continued, "Your honor, Reis is a psychiatrist and criminal psychologist. He has interviewed the defendant extensively, while simultaneously overseeing a team of specialists incorporating findings into a series of physical and psychical tests in the alpha spectrum alongside psi evalua—"

"*Thank* you, Mr. Baker." Hatch was clearly frustrated by the proceedings. "I have Dr. Reis's credits right here. He is admitted to the stand."

The bailiff opened the courtroom doors and stepped outside. Half a minute later he reappeared with a severe-looking man in a light gray suit. Reis walked with an odd limp suggesting prosthesis: his progress was slow, and his right foot seemed to tremble an instant before meeting the floor. He looked like a Nazi death camp administrator; an officious workaholic who could write you off pleasantly or spare you with indifference. That said, he was a grimly handsome man, with a salt-and-pepper crew cut and iron jaw. Vilenov stared venomously as the doctor limped down the aisle. Reis ignored him completely, steadfastly staring straight ahead. He climbed into the stand with great dignity, and with great dignity was sworn in.

"Dr. Reis," Hatch said equably, "you are chief investigator over a team of specialists specifically involved in an inquiry into the defendant's mental processes?"

"This," Reis lisped, "is a statement of fact."

Hatch looked from Abram to Baker with an almost imperceptible shake of the head. He turned back to Reis. "Rather than become immersed in a lengthy examination right now, Doctor, I'd like you to present to this court an overview of your sessions with the defendant, and a summary of your conclusions."

Reis nodded curtly. He moved back from the microphone and cleared his throat, clasped his hands on his lap. Leaning forward, he spoke to the room with the measured monotone of a man talking down a suicide.

"First of all, I want to testify that this was not a compliant subject. He resented and despised me from the outset; extracting information from Mr. Vilenov was like squeezing blood from the proverbial turnip. However, by patiently and persistently addressing his demons, which are by the way all familial, I was eventually able to attain a fairly clear picture of a most extraordinary personality."

"Go on, Doctor."

Reis appeared to brighten. "Well, Mr. Vilenov's story is one of remarkable dysfunction, and though it is rife with Old World superstition, and contains a tiresome defense of patently supernatural events, its consistency and brooding sincerity provide, in my professional opinion, the necessary clue to his bizarre temperament and behavior. His is a capital example of what I like to call *premise spin*: by *genuinely* believing in the hocus-pocus that makes up his interpretation of reality, he enables all the impossible events and ludicrous interpretations that support that interpretation to become perfectly credible."

A harsh report of chains. Before anyone could prevent it, Vilenov was halfway to his feet. "*Enough* with the 'hocus-pocus,' man! *What did I tell you?*"

Hatch sat straight up, slamming down his palms. "Officer! You *will* restrain the defendant!"

The hands were like pile drivers. That menacing voice behind him said, "Don't speak until his honor says you can." Then, in a snarling whisper, "*Now shut your fucking face!*"

Hatch was about to ream Abram when he fell into Vilenov's furious gray eyes. A great sigh broke from his lungs like a death rattle. Exercising tremendous control, he said, "You may proceed, Doctor."

Looking everywhere but at Vilenov, Reis wriggled his shoulders and took his deepest breath. "Well, the subject appears to have been overwhelmingly influenced by his father, a gothic figure performing in a traveling circus in post-war Eastern Romania. The subject's senile mother was the better half of his act, and the two made a lucrative living, and eventually a considerable fortune, by buffaloing the superstitious peasantry with magic acts, ectoplasmic inducements, séances, and the like. The woman pretended to move random objects tele-kinetically—no doubt with the assistance of her trained sons and daughter—while her husband, a man disturbing both in looks and demeanor, made a black, unforgettable show of hyp-nosis. It was very stark and primitive, and all the more effective for its crudity. Just imagine these two purely theatrical char-acters exploiting the ancient superstitions of a well-primed audience, lost in some Godforsaken field under a cold white moon. Anyway, as I understand it, the defendant's mother was a sensational magician, but his *father* was so convincing he could milk whole crowds of their valuables through suggestion alone. That is to say, he could master his subjects' psyches using only his *presence*, as though it were a weapon. Fascinating stuff. But he was too egomaniacal for his own—"

"No!" Vilenov lunged to his feet and was immediately seized in a bear hug from behind. Observers gasped in waves as security personnel and bailiffs hurried over. Vilenov stood tall. "*No*, goddamn you! There *wasn't* any magic. This is all bull-shit!" He was locked in by six strong hands. "*Your honor*," he called out, struggling while trying to hold the judge's eyes, "this witness is manipulating the facts! I've been jerked round and round by this guy. He doesn't *listen!*" Vilenov abruptly pressed his pounding temple into his shoulder. "You're all *bull*shit!"

On the penultimate syllable Reis's hands shot to his chest and his upper body lurched forward. His skull connected with a *thunk* on the stand's massive oak rail. The entire audi-ence rose with shouts of rage, fear, and bloodlust.

Hatch hammered his gavel repeatedly. "Officers! You will *bring* this court to *order!*" Vilenov was slammed down on his chair. The uniforms quickly intimidated the audience, and in less than a minute the room was contained.

Hatch left to check on a hazy, rapidly blinking Reis. He pulled back an eyelid and studied the doctor's color, checked his pulse. He excused Reis, and was just resuming the bench, staring angrily at the defense, when Vilenov overcame his pain and threw his whole soul into the judge's eyes. Hatch seemed to sink into his robes. He motioned back the restraining officer. Vilenov stood and kicked over his chair, then used his cuffed hands to heave the table on its side, producing a flurry of loose papers. The room stopped on a dime. *"Permission,"* Vilenov hissed in the echoes, "to approach the bench."

"Step forward."

He could barely walk in his shackles. A few feet from the bench he lowered his temple to his shoulder and whispered, as much to himself as to Hatch, "Man, I'm about as sick of this crap as I can be." Vilenov took a minute to control his breathing. "I've had my skull cracked open by some illiterate old fool, been betrayed by my baby, diddled by doctors, and screwed by my attorney. Otherwise, Your Wonderfulness, I'd have to say I've been treated pretty darned well." He shook his chains at the doors covering Reis's exit. "But what bugs me more than anything is having that coat hanger define my existence!" Vilenov rolled his neck. "He's history now." He smiled bitterly. "My life's been a trip, man, a stone trip. And it's time to lay it down. So you tell everybody to pay real close attention here, and to not make any noise. I've got to get this out while the moment's ripe."

Hatch inclined his head to the left. Vilenov climbed into the witness box, his restraints causing him to move like an old man. The assigned officer stepped right into the box behind him, positioning himself against the wall at arm's-length. Every time Vilenov tried to meet the officer's eyes the man deliberately turned away. Vilenov shrugged. When he was seated comfortably his gaze swept the room.

Spectators reacted with a shuffling of shoes and nervous clearing of throats. The judge leaned forward and froze, using body language to squelch even these minor, normally forgivable noises. Half a minute later he turned back to Vilenov. "All right, sir. You've got your chance."

Vilenov ignored him.

Hatch a-*hemm*ed. "I'm...*listening.*" Suddenly he felt the onset of a tremendous yawn. He raised a hand, feigning casualness. Once the hand was covering the bottom half of his face he closed his eyes and let the yawn rip.

Chapter Seven

Vilenov

"The state's inspired criminal psychologist," Vilenov said icily, "is casually rewriting my personal history; picking and choosing points that work for him, spinning the facts so my life sounds like a joke. It *isn't* a joke. I'm going to tell you all exactly what happened, and I won't fabricate a thing. And then, just in case you think you've got me up against the wall here, I'm gonna redefine for you the phrase *'captive audience'*."

His eyes were now the center of gravity for over a hundred slack faces. Vilenov began his story in a monotone, as though speaking into a machine, giving attention to descriptive detail over feeling. Gradually the color returned to his cheeks. His speech grew more buoyant when he relived certain events, but quickly bottomed out from associated headaches. Vilenov compensated with self-control, always aiming for the mean. Except for an occasional wince during a particularly troubling memory, his expression remained even and his voice cold, though at times his desire to paint an accurate picture lent his account an ascendant, almost poetic quality. There were moments of struggle with graphic imagery, and instances of calm wholly inappropriate to the violent pulse of his story. But overall, the tenor of Vilenov's narrative most closely resembled a *confession*, yet one without guilt or shame. His manacled hands now and then pulled at the thick oak rail before him, and, though his head intermittently rocked with pain, his eyes never lost their sway.

"What that moron told you about my European roots is accurate, but all the stuff about 'acts,' and 'buffaloing,' was just a bunch of crap he made up to impress you. *He* wasn't there; *I* was." He took a deep breath.

"*Yes*, my parents were performers in a Romanian circus; *yes*, I emigrated illegally; *yes*, I've spent my entire adult life haunting the mean streets of Surf City, U.S.A. My mother died in Lodz; Father went up in smoke right here in Venice. Grandmother, Dimitri—the whole family's in the ground.

"Well, let's see now…the old man was a cold son of a bitch, known in the business as…how do I anglicize it…we didn't have a word for mesmerist—let's just call him 'the Great Mikhail,' and leave it at that. A human magnet, able to attract a crowd anywhere. But not by *trying* to, mind you, just by being nearby. Mikhail was the show's feature attraction when he met my mother, Marta, in a village outside Brasov. He was so impressed with her bang-up telekinesis act that he married her on the spot, and induced the owner to hire her on. From then on he was her personal manager and barker.

"If ever there was a union made in Hell—to hear Grandmother tell it, things got ugly right off the bat with those two. Any place the coaches stopped there'd be trouble. Customers took to brawling under the moon, women broke out in catfights and lewd displays. The emotion passed, back and forth, between my parents and the crowd, gaining in steam as the performances wore on. Mother grew able to topple distant objects with great violence. Father became the epicenter of the whole countryside's rage. People hated them. They *feared* them. But they kept coming back. And all the while Mikhail's hold was increasing dramatically. Especially his hold on women.

"You see, my old man had this absolutely ferocious sexual appetite; he must have spent half his life dodging angry husbands and fathers. His method was crude, but effective: he'd simply approach women out of the blue, bump right up on them, and envelop them in what good ol' Doctor Reis rightly termed 'his presence.' Father went on like this, brazenly, even after he'd married Marta. She gave him two sons, Dimitri and Constantine, and a daughter, Elena. When things got too close he influenced the show's owner to outfit him with a larger, finer living coach, and for a number of years they all traveled like royalty, relatively speaking.

"In time Mikhail grew so influential he didn't need to perform. All he had to do was hold a customer in his sway and the guy would gladly turn over the deed to his farm. A great deal of riches rolled in over the years; gold and silver, precious stones and jewelry—all stashed beneath the floorboards of that splendid coach. By then Father and Mother could easily have made it on their own, but they elected to stay with the troupe. Circus crowds were still the best bet.

"Fame was honey to Father's ego. Success made him brasher and brasher; soon he was taking the peasant girls in plain sight. Who knows how many poor bastards that monster produced. The man was insatiable.

"Anyway, I was born sometime in the mid-sixties. Father and Mother were both in their fifties, and still going strong. Dimitri had taken a wife; a fourteen year-old farm girl named Kirin. Mikhail was regularly violating his own daughter Elena, so she and Constantine flew the coop, deciding they'd rather live with the wolves than with the devil. That left Father, Mother, Dimitri, and Kirin; a family quickly rearranged upon my birth, for Mother, tough and fertile as she was, couldn't handle the strain of childbirth at her age. Her death was a crushing blow to gentle Dimitri, but it wasn't any skin off Father. Before she was even in the ground he was working on Kirin.

"Dimitri freaked. One black night, with wine in his belly, he caught them in the act and took a saber to the old man. The next morning Dimitri was found in an open field; his guts cut out by that same saber, and by his own hand.

"Locals were spooked by the rumors. And now, with his dark name blackened even further, the Great Mikhail's business was falling off correspondingly. He grew increasingly distant and restless, finally setting off upon the Carpathians in that magnificent coach, with only me and Kirin, to seek fresh meat. I still have vivid memories of clopping along in the darkness, bundled up between that silent oak of a man and his shell-shocked plaything. Before I was nine years old I was a total mess.

"It was in the vicinity of Cluj-Napoca that Father, hav-

ing just influenced a group of American tourists out of their lug-
gage and cash, had an experience that radically changed his life,
and indirectly led to all you lovely, law-abiding ladies and gentlemen, sitting with me so patiently in this wonderful room. But
it will seem such a *trivial* event.

"What Father found at the bottom of a pinched suitcase
was a single postcard, posted from Venice Beach, right here in
sunny Southern California. I distinctly recall my first-and-only
glimpse, and remember understanding, subliminally, that no human being other than he was ever to view it again.

"The postcard's face was a glossy, full-color photograph
of six bronzed, nearly nude beach bunnies frolicking in the surf
with a bright red Frisbee. This card just blew my father's mind.
For weeks he was severely depressed and withdrawn; couldn't
speak, couldn't eat, couldn't screw. The peasant girls became
slime to him, and Kirin just another homely pig. He never spoke
of it, but I felt his resolve as he hurried our horses west. Mikhail
was a man on a mission.

"He sold the horses and coach in Hungary, and we took
a train for Portugal. Father didn't trust currency, so he made us
drag satchels stuffed with gold wherever we went. He didn't
need it; he could take what he wanted. But he wasn't letting go
of his hoard. The Great Mikhail answered only to the Grim
Reaper. Also, he was dead-on in his assessment of humanity.
The flash of gold moved men far quicker than the application of
his will.

"In Lisbon we boarded an enormous steamer. For two
weeks Father was a walking time bomb; seasick one day, un-
bearably restless the next. The endless ocean was a terrible blow
to his ego. He lost all sexual appetite, and, strange now that I
think about it, it was the only time I've seen women repelled by
him. When he got cabin fever he'd storm on deck, scattering
passengers and coalescing the crew. Everybody would watch in
dead silence while he stood at the bow; his tall, wind-blown
shape standing out against the horizon like a gnarly prow. Finally he'd stomp back down to our cabin and lose himself in
that damned postcard.

"Soon as we disembarked in New York the tiger was out
of his cage. Reinvigorated by all the hookers and strip clubs,

Father sold pounds of gold and jewelry for quick American cash, but his manners and appearance were just too profane. In Albuquerque the law came down on us. We were run out of town on a rail, so to speak; Father bundled us onto a train and we began our long, eye-popping journey across this beautiful country.

"He'd learned from his New York experiences. When we reached Los Angeles he managed to control his urges, though the sight of bikinis, the smell of suntan oil, and the sudden feel of a bright baking sun just tore him up. He bought a gothic, two-storied house in Old Venice, halfway down Wave Crest between Speedway and Pacific. Not two blocks from the beach, only half a mile from the Canals. He was drawn to this sagging old place, I suppose, because it reminded him of the rambling structures back home.

"He really fell in love with that old Ocean Front Walk in Venice; you could tell the carnival-like atmosphere brought back his showman's memories. Father, with his huge graying beard and flowing black robes, blended right in. Street artists had a field day with him, and pretty soon his likeness was popping up everywhere; on silk-screened T-shirts, on posters, on canvases. Kids mimicked his long gliding gait, little schoolgirls ran screaming with their hands tucked between their legs. Father himself grew less and less anxious, though he'd never allow his picture taken, or engage in any conversation beyond grunts and monosyllables. It wasn't just that his grasp of English was so limited. He could have learned, in time. But he was too busy for distractions. He was looking, always looking.

"Mikhail began bringing home some of the loveliest, least-clad bunnies he could find, and introducing them into his stable. Initially there was this big confused outrage in our neighborhood, but when it came right down to it nobody really wanted a piece of him; a look from Father was like ice on your heart. This strange, brooding tension hung over Wave Crest. Neighbors went about their lives without humor or interest, letting their houses fall apart and their yards go to hell. Wave Crest is actually a walk, not a street, maybe ten feet wide. There are lots of trees. Those trees were allowed to grow together overhead, cutting out the sun. Inside this dreary tunnel, if you had the balls

to peep through your blinds, you just might see my father silently gliding along with a clinging, shivering bunny. And then
you'd turn away and forget what you saw, and the bogeyman
and his bunny would disappear into the bowels of the huge dilapidated two-story.

"It was a suffocating atmosphere for an eleven year-old
boy, a grim sex freeway. At any time there may have been eight
or nine women living in our house, and Father, true to form,
made no secret of his activities. I couldn't pass a day without
seeing him going at it like a dog.

"But it was during this period that he began to show a
real paternal interest in me. Never spoke, never gestured; just
made his points with looks of approval or disapproval. He commanded Grandmother to educate me, in our native tongue, on
the manifold glories of his black career and filthy conquests.
Soon he grew sick of her plodding, and, I think, sick of his own
ignorance. He began coming home not only with bunnies, but
with school teachers. These women were engaged in my education from the ground up, and they were totally devoted to my
progress. The English language was drilled into my brain. I was
kept prisoner in a book-lined room, schooled relentlessly by one
after the other. I had literally hundreds of 'mothers' over those
few years, hand-picked to educate me by leaps and bounds in
the sciences, in literature, in philosophy. Once a 'mother's' potential was exhausted, she was disposed of and never seen a-
gain, replaced by a new 'mother' able to school me at a higher
level. I was force-fed a quality, rounded education, entirely a-
gainst my will. But *you*, who've never experienced this man's
will, don't know how effective his looks could be. His eyes impaled you, absorbed you, *commanded* you. And so I learned.

"One powerful lesson I took from this succession of
'mothers' didn't come by way of books. When I hit puberty a
change came in my studies. My 'mothers' rapidly became more
physical, then seriously groping, then urgently sexual. At first I
was bewildered by the unblinking passion of their advances,
and thought only of hiding. But the constant *cramming*—the
books, the commands, the encouragement—had taught me to
think. Father's influence, especially over women, became my
whole focus. I got into some heavy studies at night, locked in

that drafty room with a flashlight and a thousand books. I brooded over biochemical catalysts and adaptive functions, thought long and hard about the forces directing propagation, and ended up with an insider's view of certain related phenomena which aren't normally cross-referenced, simply because they seem so obviously *unrelated*. I walked the line between science and the occult; reading extensively on the natural and the supernatural, and cataloguing rumors of the paranormal— rumors considered basic facts in the Old World for centuries. I discovered things, man; things you candy Christians will never know. Clairvoyance, mind reading, communication with animals...these aren't magic powers! Freaks, I was fast catching on, are glandular superhighways.

"And I learned of peoples and cultures throughout history, noting the normal range of behavior and appetite. I'd had an epiphany, one of many: my studies on androgenic processes, and especially on pheromones, came at a point in my development when I was beginning to realize my father had to be the horniest man to ever live. You see, it's all about procreation. That's what the so-called 'meaning of life' is. It struck me, even then, that the ability to stimulate the opposite sex is one of the stronger forces in animal nature, and that those individuals possessing this *procreative virtue* in the greatest degree will produce more offspring, and so further their strain. I'm not stupid, man. I know it's all just a great big stampede of hormones. The crux of reproduction is quantity, not quality. Evolution isn't 'survival of the fittest,' for Christ's sake. In the long run, linearly, it's survival of the most prolific. *They* are the cream of the crop. I got this idea of a natural channel; like a sieve, if you can picture it, that singles out highly specialized individuals, bringing the most audacious creations to the fore, to a finer, less 'polluted' state. This notion might seem a little strange in this fine, upstanding courthouse—that the best specimen is the least democratic, that in raw nature *lack of restraint* is a tremendous asset.

"*Trends* are disseminated, okay? The herd passes them along in their offspring. Over many generations, they define the herd's general behavior, general direction, general appetite. But in a *single line*, also after many generations, this same process

83

can produce *traits*. Follow me here: a pack leader is not a pack leader because, out of all members in the pack, this leader just *happens* to be the specimen best suited for the position. A pack leader is an individual genetically groomed for the job, through innumerable generations of very specialized pack leaders. But the strain must be kept as *pure* as possible, through the 'in-breeding,' if you will, of exemplary specimens. *Listen*, you clueless Gumbies: in our own time a president, a general, or a CEO, is not a specimen 'best suited for the job!' In that super-achiever's blood courses the rage, the lust, and the indomitable spirit of super-achievers long wed to the dust. The greatest genealogist on this planet might not be able to detect the lineal connection, but it's there. And all these super-specimens may croak early because of their excesses, and not leave a trace.

"Except in their seed.

"And I recognized Father as the bearer of an antediluvian torch; perhaps the sole representative of some primitive stock that didn't *mutate* for the good of the herd, or die out as a useless anomaly, but actually *evolved*—if I dare use the word—in virility, in *herd-sway*, generation by generation, along a very specialized, and very effective line. It made me curse all my studies, made me sweat in my dreams, because the next freak in line was Yours Truly! It totally scared the shit out of me. You see, despite a healthy desire to love and be loved, I loathed that man from the bottom of my heart. No way did I want to become *him*.

"Like a physical blow, I saw my parents' union as a perfectly *inevitable coincidence*. They were part of a collateral line. Both were highly specialized individuals. Both embodied primitive traits melded and focused to the nth degree. And I was their product. Man, it was in my frigging genes! I tried telling myself that I'd been thinking too hard, that I'd got hold of what must seem, to all you glass-eyed dummies, an absolutely silly idea. But this silly idea was made more and more believable by the increasingly wild advances of my 'mothers.'

"I was my father's son, no doubt about it. Mikhail's women were paying ever closer attention, fondling me, tearing at me, while his jealousy simmered. Even Grandmother showed signs of affection that were not strictly 'family.'

"You see, when I was younger, and especially during this string of 'mothers,' it had been convenient for clarity's sake that Mikhail instill in Kirin a penchant for calling herself 'grandmother,' and myself 'grandson.' These became our pet names for each other, and, in time, our general understanding. In the end nothing could have convinced me otherwise, for Kirin sure looked the part. She was only twenty-eight, but Father's incessant sexual assaults made her appear sixty.

"And her advances became less and less subtle with each passing day, until one summer morning I woke up flat on my back, straddled by this naked, burned-out hag. She was out of her mind with lust. Before I even knew what was doing, the door burst open to reveal Father's hunched silhouette, trimmed in rose by the first rays of dawn.

"Mikhail bashed her over and over with a twisted old poker from the front room hearth. He struck her like a man laying into a snake, then chased her screaming and spurting around the room until she collapsed against the wall, half-buried in tumbled books. He turned on me slowly, raising the bloody poker high, but I instinctively threw a hand over my eyes, grabbed my pants, and blindly dashed from the room.

"I remember running along the beach...hiding in the handball courts at Muscle Beach...running crying through yards...trying to ditch him at the Canals. But it seemed I couldn't turn without seeing him; all black robes and salt-and-pepper beard, gliding somberly in the morning fog while tapping that poker like a blind man. At times he would freeze in my direction, and I'd cringe as he stood there, feeling the area. But he was never able to locate me, and I became convinced he was only hip to my whereabouts when I was on the move. So I stayed put and out-waited him, pushing myself deeper into the embankment under a pretty little painted bridge, holding my breath while ducks and tiny crabs cruised and clambered beside me.

"After a while Mikhail touched the poker to the ground, picking up vibrations. He moved left and right with infinite slowness, sensing all around. Slowly, slowly he turned to face the bridge, staring very hard. The poker rose almost imperceptibly, until it pointed directly between my eyes.

"But his concentration was broken by a jogger, puffing across a street-to-canal walkway between two old houses. When my father turned back he was rattled. He cursed, raised the poker high overhead, and shook it in silent rage. Instantly a small tethered rowboat writhed on the water, and a front room window erupted into a thousand shards.

"He began moving back toward home, the neighborhood dogs howling insanely at his approach, and whining like kittens once he'd passed. I continued watching him glide along, pausing every hundred yards or so to inspect the area, until at last he passed out of sight.

"That whole morning I walked the beach north, always keeping to the waterline. I was out of my mind with fear, because I knew Father would kill me when he found me. I *knew* it. You who've never been under his influence will never understand what I'm rapping about here. You're *chilled*; chilled to the marrow. That man's shadow weighed a ton. So I walked with my feet in the surf; I'd already resolved to throw myself under the waves and drown the instant I felt him near. I walked all the way to Malibu before I finally fell on the sand and cried like a baby. I spent the whole day there, hiding from the sun, thinking about my situation. And I realized my life was over. I'd never be able to sleep. I'd always be afraid I'd wake and find him looming over me, his eyes burning like coals. Not until late afternoon did I begin the long walk home.

"When I came within a mile of our house it was twilight. I found myself loitering around the open back door of a mom-and-pop hardware store, going through these little panic attacks. Then, without even thinking about it, I stepped inside and picked up a gallon can of kerosene. The huge shadow of the owner fell on me, and I remember wilting, and our eyes meeting.

"Now a really strange thing happened. This guy gently disengaged the can and placed it back on the shelf, took my little hand and led me a ways down the aisle. He picked out four cans of Coleman lantern fuel and set them by my feet, walked to the front counter and returned with an oversized brown paper bag, placed the fuel in the bag, and the bag in my arms. I then followed him around the store, stopping beside him whenever he paused to pick something off a shelf and deposit it in the bag. He dropped in a box of strike-anywhere matches and a carton of those long wooden fireplace matches, added a sparker for barbecues, a long-nosed butane lighter, Sterno cans, a propane canister, and a handful of emergency candles. When he reached for the charcoal I realized there was no logic to his actions, just a robotic compulsion that caused him to grab anything under the category of *combustibles*.

"I stood there in the aisle, blinking wonderingly at him. After a minute he seemed to feel my hesitation, led me back out the rear entrance and gently closed the door.

"For a while I leaned against a trash bin with the stuffed bag in my arms, then slowly made my way home. I patiently squeezed through a break in the alley fence and crouched in the backyard bushes, as motionless as a lawn jockey. The lights were on, upstairs and down, and I knew Father was having his way with his stable. I didn't move. At ten o'clock the lights went off and the house settled in for the night. I willed myself to stone; refusing to yawn, refusing even to blink.

"Around midnight the back screen door opened silently, and my father's high black silhouette glided out onto the dilapidated rear porch, seemingly without moving a muscle. He gripped the sagging rail and waited. He must have stood there motionlessly for an hour or more, embroidered by bougainvillea and night blooming jasmine, utilizing God knows what senses. Finally his head began turning with extreme slowness. He was *feeling* the yard. As the plane of his gaze approached mine I took a chance and closed my eyes as gently as possible, lest the brushing of my lashes seize his attention.

"I'm not sure how long I crouched there. I remember cautiously opening my eyes to find the back porch vacated, but not until three a.m. did I find the courage to unbend my legs. Now, I knew Father was a very heavy sleeper. Even so, I spent another fifteen minutes creeping up to his bedroom window.

"Like most windows in Venice on hot summer nights, ours were wide open. I very carefully poured Coleman fuel all along the sill so that it trickled down the inner and outer walls. Then I moved around the house, soaking the sills and drenching the curtains. After splashing Coleman on the doors and porches,

I crept around a second time, lighting curtains, sills and porches with those long fireplace matches. I torched the house.

"I didn't give a damn about the old man's innocent harem. All I know is I ran. I ran as if the Devil were after me, and didn't stop until I heard distant sirens. A bright rage of flame was leaping over Wave Crest.

"I slept under Santa Monica Pier that night. When I woke, hungry and scared, I was amazed to find beachgoers offering me more food and money than I could handle, and without a word on my part. I'd come of age! Wherever I went, people *bent* to me. At first it wasn't all that radical, but it *developed.* And once I was comfortable with it I slept in the plushest hotels, and ate gourmet meals until I was sick of 'em.

"Yet there were drawbacks. A moment of anger or fear, and weird crap would happen. If I got pissed at any little thing there'd be a physical consequence somewhere nearby. Maybe a clock would fall off a wall, maybe a chair would tip over. Or maybe some prying son of a bitch would suffer sudden stabbing pains. I began experimenting. Soon I was producing violent temporary changes in my immediate environment; I was literally walking around in a sphere of influence. When I first got into it, even when really concentrating, I could only slightly affect very small objects within a few yards. But I remember right now, as clearly as I remember breakfast, this intense little boy standing on the beach before sunrise…scattering gulls by desire alone…setting small fires in trash heaps, just by *willing* it so. And I see him growing into manhood, and I see him walking through the world taking anything he wanted, and I see him making life just a tad more miserable for all you recurrent assholes.

"*And* assholes…*assholes*—when I was fifteen, or maybe only fourteen—I began exploiting the tender, the succulent, the *easy* buffet of Woman. Are you *listening?* I did your wife, Mister Everyman, and I'll do your mother, too. I'll do your daughter, I'll do your niece, I'll do your goddamned fucking bitch dog if I feel like it! Just like I did everybody I ever wanted, whether they wanted it or not. You trust me on this: my life has been one long plunge into pussy. And you know what? I didn't care if they were married, or pregnant, or on the rag. Or whether they were on their way to grade school or the senior center. As long as they were *packaged*. You know what I mean? Every man knows what I mean. As long as they had the right stuff. In the right places.

"I've had *thousands* of women, man…*tens* of thousands. I spent my teens, my twenties, my thirties…doing whatever I wanted! Doing what every man wants. When I was broke I just walked into any store and had the clerk hand me some cash. When I got hungry or sleepy it was a simple matter of ordering. And when I got horny, man, when I saw a hefty pair jiggling and wiggling down the strand, I didn't have to almost pass out with desire like you losers. I'd have that bikini off in *no time*, and be right back in paradise! Are you paying attention, *ass*-holes? Is any of this getting through to you? I can make any of your bitches do whatever I want, just as I can make any of *you* do whatever I want. Just as I can make you see and remember what I *want* you to see and remember.

"You all think this is some kind of real-time drama go-ing on here, don't you? You think your homespun righteousness is just gonna come crashing down like a virtuous wall, and de-stroy me for indulging in the very activity you've spent half your lives fantasizing about. You think I'll be punished for what I've done with my blind luck. Just like you believe your ship's coming in, just like you believe your God's so bored He'd give a crap about a pissant like you, just like you believe your half-assed Constitution *proves* all the freak products of existence gravitate into some lukewarm puddle where nobody gets any more than anybody else. But it doesn't work like that. Life is a cruel crapshoot that favors the outrageous. And what's *really* going to happen is this:

"I'm gonna walk out of here in triumph, the vindicated victim of your funky white witch hunt. I'll be a free man again! Because your honor-my ass is about to rule I've been hounded by the cops, unjustly incarcerated, and caged like a wild animal for the sake of public opinion. Not only that, he's gonna apolo-gize for all the trouble this state, and you people, have caused me, and he's gonna *mean it!* Plus, he'll make damn sure I get out of this pesthole without being screwed by that mob of geeks out there. And my self-serving counsel, before he tries to get out of Dodge with the shitload of cash he's ripped from me, will take it doggy-style from my new buddy Orin here, in full view of this court. Then the DA, once I look him in the eyes, will get on his knees, kiss my hairy white ass, and bow out of office permanently. And the rest of you meatballs? Book deals, movie contracts, speaking engagements? Is that what you're all thinking? Well, you'd better dream while you can. Because as soon as I train one of your goons to get these chains off me, I'm gonna march right back in, and I'm gonna tear you all to pieces; slowly, exquisitely, as creatively as I can.

"Don't mistake me here. You're under my influence. The judgment of this court will be in my favor, and each and every one of you will sing my praises. And even as you're singing I'll be prodding you and probing you and carving you up like the turkeys you are. And you'll like it. Because I'll *tell* you to like it. You're all sucking whores and frauds." Vilenov smacked his palm twice on the oak rail, imitating a gavel-rapping judge. "I rest my case. Your Majesty, you may proceed."

And the huge yawn passed, allowing Hatch to just as nonchalantly remove his hand. "Apparently Mr. Vilenov," he sighed, "is unwilling to communicate after all." He took off his glasses, massaged the bridge of his nose with forefinger and thumb. When he looked back up his expression was deadly. "This court finds no alternative to ordering the immediate release of defendant Nicolas Vilenov. The District Attorney's office has been overzealous in this matter, and has allowed due process to take a back seat to public opinion. The defendant was unjustly incarcerated. From the outset the state's case has relied on physical evidence that cannot be corroborated by eyewitness testimony, and circumstantial evidence that is dubious at best. Mr. Vilenov, his name sullied, was carted through the streets of L.A. like a caged wild animal. It is the prayer of this court that his release will in some measure be vindication for the victim of a modern witch hunt. For the State of California in general, and for the people of Los Angeles County in particular, I apologize from the bottom of my heart. Mr. Vilenov, your entry into this usually august chamber was an ignominious event, and a real danger to your physical and spiritual well-being. For your safety you will be escorted from the building through an alternate entrance." He tapped his gavel twice. "This is now a civil matter. You are a free man again."

"Get up," said the officer behind Vilenov. "Get up, very quietly, and march your ass to the door."

Vilenov rose unsteadily, his chains clanking about him. The officer, spooning right up, grabbed him by the nape and a bicep. "I thought I said 'quietly'!"

"Can do," Vilenov grunted. "*Sir*. But let's waltz out of here like a couple of winners, shall we? We can discuss our differences in the corridor." He tried to look back as he was shoved from the room, but could only make out the badge and nametag. "Welcome to Manners 101, officer...Welle, is it? Well, Welle, pay real close attention here. Professor Vilenov's in the house."

"Now," said Hatch, staring coldly at Abram, "I think it's time we cleared up a little smoke. Generally speaking, a defendant in my court is acquitted on the strength of the evidence and his counsel's arguments. Rarely have I seen a client less ably served. Mr. Abram, in your many years as an extremely successful defense attorney you have, to my knowledge, never compromised your integrity. But you sure seem to have gone out of your way today. As I mentioned earlier, I view the courtroom as a solemn and virtuous place. It is not a forum for well-heeled sophists. When Mr. Vilenov took the stand, desperate to interject a clear voice yet unable to utter a word, I couldn't help but feel he was tongue-tied because of the confusion you'd sown."

"Your honor," Abram managed, "I am no less confused. I've spent endless hours preparing Mr. Vilenov to speak in his own be—"

"Counsel, you'll hold your tongue!"

Abram dropped his head as though facing a firing squad. Hatch went on with mounting fury, pounding his gavel like an overseer beating time in a slave galley. "In *case* you haven't *noticed*, Mr. *Abram*, you are being *admonished* here. You have *embarrassed* this *court* and made a *mockery* of the *Bar!*" He caught his breath and dropped the gavel. His face was quite red. "Now go on. Get out of my courtroom before I forget who and where I am. Be advised that you will not humiliate the legal profession before me again." He pushed himself to his feet, and without another word stormed from the room.

In dead silence the bailiff mumbled, "Everybody rise."

Lawrence Abram snapped shut his briefcase, the reports resonating like the double-slam of a paramedic's van. He marched through the doors and out the building, his briefcase in front of his head, his face down. To the army of reporters he had only one comment, which was "No comment." For a crazy minute he was flailing; drowning in a sea of pleading humanity. But there was a sound beacon: he heard the *dot dash dot dot, dot dash* of a car's horn, Morse for *LA*, Larry Abram. He worked in the sound's direction until he found Dottie waiting, the door open and the Lexus humming. Abram jumped in and slammed the door. He sank low in the seat, burying his head in court papers as the car slowly pressed back the crowd.

That bright white light was going to burn right through his eyelids if he didn't turn his head. Vilenov moved only a millimeter and his temple screamed with pain. He froze, closing his eyes even tighter. He could survive the light. But at that moment he'd have rather died than repeat the agony.

There was a stirring near his feet. Low voices. A narrow head eclipsed the light.

"Good morning, asshole," the head said pleasantly. The light, a high-watt bulb centered in an inverted stainless steel bowl, was swung aside to reveal the sneering face of Vincent Beasely.

Vilenov's eyes desperately sought reference.

He was flat on his back, strapped to a table in an oblong storeroom for medical equipment. Along the wall to his left, a stainless steel counter held tagged syringes, gauze wraps, and scalpels folded in sterilized towels. The room reeked of antiseptics. A man wearing a white smock was leaning against the closed door, his hairy arms folded across his chest. Heavy black eyeglasses perched halfway down his nose as he peered at the waking confrontation. Beasely was stepping back and forth behind Vilenov's head with all the fire of a Rottweiler taunted by a trespasser.

"That was a really pretty speech you gave in the court-room, pigface. I know, because I was standing in the transfer corridor with my ear against the door the whole time. And when you were brought out I gave you *such* a whack on the temple, man—man, I hit you so hard you're not gonna be able to screw anybody for a long, long time. I did it right, too. Just before the trial the gallant Doctor Reis showed me exactly where to strike the temple, and exactly how hard, using only a trusty nightstick. A little *too* hard and I could have killed you. But that would've spoiled all the fun. Besides, you're already a dead man. But not walking." Beasely reached to his left and rocked a gurney back and forth. "You're a dead man rolling." He leaned forward, his garlicky breath suffocating.

"Now it's time to give you the lowdown on some radical news I just know you're gonna find real interesting. Dig: *you were never slated to go roamin' again*, horn-dog! Never! You're back in the criminal ward of Western State Hospital, where you were rushed by ambulance immediately following your unfortunate accident in the corridor. We'll get those steps fixed yet.

"I don't know if you realize just how fascinating you are to a whole lot of people, *punk*; some who want to see you dead right away, some who aren't in such a hurry. There's a big team of specialists on this ward who aren't at all satisfied with your pre-trial results, and these guys have put their heads together. They've decided to do a little experimenting. On the side, if you know what I mean." He winked. "And guess what? *These guys don't like you either!*"

At the bottom of his vision, Vilenov saw the police surgeon slowly shake his head. The signal was unnecessary; he wasn't so messed up he'd believe in an underground conspiracy of mad doctors. The only genuine lunatic was right in his face.

"Look, you're not gonna be offed first, okay? That's way too good for the likes of you. And it's way too traumatic an event for the organs. Gas, juice, rope, or injection—any of these procedures could end up damaging whatever freak biological factor makes you tick, and above all else the medical community is passionately interested in slowly, thoroughly checking you out, piece by piece. They don't want any overwhelming shock to the system, see? And no jolt to the brain." He rubbed his palms together. "So what's gonna happen is this. You're gonna be kept alive artificially, and your heart, if we can find one, is gonna be very carefully extracted for study. But before that the surgeons are gonna slice you open like a ripe cantaloupe, man, and carefully, methodically remove your organs one by one for analysis while the equipment keeps you alive. This *can* be done! Oh yeah; make no mistake about it. Pumps, respirators, dialysis, transfusions—a virtually organ-less man *can* be kept alive, and *conscious*, and *suffering*, for the longest time, depending on the quality of the facilities and specialists. And we'll have only the best: *we're gonna keep you going forever, freak!* We're gonna violate you just like you violated all those poor, helpless, beautiful young women. Only you're gonna be alert while it happens. Kidneys, stomach, pancreas, lungs—all cut out of the mute, horrified monster and transferred to Hotel Formaldehyde." He shivered with delicious anticipation. "But first they're gonna cut off your balls, creep. I've got a front row seat for that one. Reason is they think androgens may be responsible. I heard your rap about pheromones and whatnot, muskrat, and you may be right. The brainiacs'll find out, sooner or later. Pituitary is a big draw here too, along with the hypothalamus, but they can't dig into your gray matter until your body's dead and your filthy soul's been consigned to whatever level of Hell the lowest form of prick is shoveled into. And when you get there, shit-pile, say 'hi' to Adolf, Charlie, and Kenny B. for me. You'll be in illustrious company."

The surgeon took a step forward and placed a pacifying hand on Beasely's shoulder. Beasely shook it off.

"And I'm gonna be a *real* bad boy, dickhead; the worst I can be. I'm gonna make *sure* I go to Hell, just so's I can come looking for you!"

The surgeon moved behind Beasely, clamped his hands on the man's biceps. "All right, Vince, he's got the picture."

But Beasely went on, straining against the hold until his face and Vilenov's were inches apart. The veins on Beasely's forehead stood out like snakes. Vilenov's raging gray eyes bulged in their sockets.

"I'll cut you to pieces!" Beasely screamed, dragging the police surgeon right down on top of them. "I'll bend you over a sink and screw your lights out with a baseball bat! I'll bash you into the grave! I'll bash you into eternity!" Beasely completely ignored the surgeon straddling his back, even though the man was yelling straight into his ear: "I said that's *enough*, Vinnie, *that's enough!"*

Vilenov's eyes broke from his tormentor's and locked with the straining surgeon's. The man, heroically fighting Vilenov's influence, nevertheless drew his clasped arms up Beasely's chest until he had him by the throat. There was a moment when everything seemed to freeze. Beasely's eyes rolled back in his skull and he squealed like a hare in a gray wolf's fangs. Suddenly the police surgeon lunged off the locked bodies and leaped to the polished counter against the wall. He spun around with a fistful of scalpels, jumped on Beasely and began plunging the blades into the shrieking man's back.

Even when the mob of security and medical personnel came stomping in, the police surgeon continued to hack and slice. They tore him off the pressed bodies and wrestled him out into the hall. Two security men and a nurse, badly cut, had to be rushed to the emergency room.

And even after Beasely's all but eviscerated body was covered, and the purple, writhing prisoner had been wheeled out of the trashed and bespattered room, it still took two interns, a third security officer, and the near-hysterical admissions nurse to restrain the blood-soaked, jerking right arm of the spewing police surgeon.

Chapter Eight

The Fugitive

Sweet Harbor restaurant is a castaway's mansion snuggled in a lush grove of palms.

Customers entering off the driftwood-bordered parking lot cross a wide, rope-railed wood bridge swallowed up in a fern-and-bamboo tunnel. This bridge, cleverly constructed to give the impression of a dilapidated structure on the verge of collapse, spans an artificial pond stocked with goldfish the size of roof rats.

The establishment's rear is built entirely of glass, offering diners cloudless skies, breathtaking sunsets, and an unobstructed view of yachts rocking side by side in Marina del Rey's Basin F. On the broad sundeck you'll find faded canvas umbrellas for daytime, tall gas heaters for that occasional nippy California night, leaning tiki torches and strung globe candles, glass-topped wicker tables, leather-padded chairs, and one very paranoid tourist working hard on his third Piña Colada.

Abram's disguise, while comical, was effective: a loud Hawaiian shirt, Bermuda shorts, dark knee-high dress socks and brown wingtips. Heavy shades under a silk-banded Homburg featuring pins of an American flag, a smiley face, and a terribly abashed Betty Boop. All he needed was a camera slung round his neck to complete the picture of a Wisconsin geek searching for Disneyland.

To the staff of Sweet Harbor, the defense attorney's isolation was perfectly understandable—his mood was so down his very presence had swept the deck. And to Nelson Prentis, standing inside watching his friend through the glass, Abram's depression was as clear as the powder blue sky. The man was a loser.

The discrepancies in court-recorded and actual time, Judge Hatch's inexplicable fiery admonition, and the vague admissions of mysterious headaches and general confusion reported by the audience, were all delightful breaks for the four o'clock news. Abram was hit hardest, certainly, but he was seasoned enough to handle it with grace and good humor. Hatch, sincerely unable to account for his behavior, apologized personally and publicly in a much-discussed news conference, rebroadcast nationally every hour, and locally every quarter hour. A thorough investigation of each man and woman in that courtroom was already under way.

To the rest of the country the post-trial telecast was a scrumptiously over-produced vision of La-la land as Bedlam— all opinions of a state long-considered flaky, spoiled, and downright incompetent were reaffirmed in spades. But in L.A. itself the Vilenov circus only gained steam; in certain circles the man was already painlessly morphing from monster to cult hero. And Abram, seen over most of his career as a symbol of flash and arrogance, was suddenly a champion of the little guy. There were calls from breathless women on his answering machine, proposals for top-paying interviews in his email. Prompt service at the market and dry cleaners, thumbs-ups from strangers on the street. At first merely amused, he quickly grew exhilarated by all the attention.

But the news of Beasely's murder was an instant crash and burn. Though there wasn't a single professional or lay theory that could adequately account for the surgeon's sudden psychotic behavior, Abram had a theory of his own: his ex-client had been telling the truth in their first interview, and was able to get back at his enemies indirectly, through some means not scientifically explainable. Abram cancelled all appointments and turned off his answering machine, embraced his family and had a long conversation with his rabbi.

That night at nine, Nicolas Vilenov's second escape hit the South Bay like a tsunami. Abram began drinking recklessly and smashed his answering machine, became argumentative with his family and rabbi, and locked himself in his basement office. His rambling phone calls tapered to incoherence. Eventually he passed out.

Some time after one a.m., Lawrence Abram lurched to his senses and went for his wife's throat. Barbara threw the kids in the car and vanished. Nelson Prentis, monitoring the red-eye Houdini-rapist Task Force, took her hysterical call half an hour later. Prentis had yet to catch a moment's sleep.

This would all make for a tense encounter anywhere else, and between almost any other two people. But both men had spent countless hours here, and Prentis's affection for Abram went way deeper than simple friendship. He could forgive Abram anything. Under these heaters and umbrellas, the men had developed an immutable professional understanding: their career paths, by definition adversarial, ended at the office. Here cases were discussed with honesty, with compassion, and with balls. And confidence is sacred between friends.

Prentis crossed the deck arm-in-arm with his favorite waitress, cranking up the volume on his small talk to herald his coming. But Abram, staring miserably into his empty glass, was so far gone he didn't realize he had company until their shadows leaped on his folded arms.

"Easy, buddy! Take it easy. Nelson Prentis, remember? Childhood, adulthood; stuff like that."

Abram wiped his palms on his Bermudas. "Sorry, Nellie. I guess I was kind of zoned out there."

"So I noticed."

The pretty blonde waitress beamed like the sun breaking through clouds. Prentis ordered another Piña Colada for Abram, and for himself a tall glass of Ancient Age with Schweppes Bitter Lemon over ice, crowned by a slice of lime, chipped honey, and a short handful of maraschinos. His fingernails tapped the glass tabletop in an accelerating crescendo, an old law school habit. It was his personal drum roll.

"I've got news, Larry; the good, the bad, and the ugly. First, the good. I've been on and off the phone with Babs all morning. She's with the kids at her mom's place. Everybody's fine."

Abram sagged. "So you know."

"All about it. Look, I could see you were taking the news hard when you left all those messages, but what made you take it out on Babs?"

Abram could only shake his head. He looked away.

Prentis waited.

Finally Abram shook his head again. The waitress brought their drinks. Prentis signed for the tab, folded the receipt and placed it in his shirt's pocket.

Abram took a quick swallow, the sun dancing on his shades. "So how did he walk? Damn it, Nelson, you *assured* me his cell was tight!"

"So I did, and so it was. After he was released from emergency with nothing worse than a nasty bruise on his temple, Vilenov was given a series of tranquilizers and placed in a special cell designed to hold even the most dangerous prisoners." He looked at Abram very directly. "For his own protection, of course."

"He was put in a rubber room?"

"Pretty much. But without the jacket. Vilenov was about as mellow as a man can be under the circumstances. At 7:10 the video has him facing the door, and shows the guard looking at him through the peephole." Again with the drum roll. "Larry, this goes a lot deeper than we thought. It can't be substantiated, of course, but Vilenov appears to have somehow influenced the guard with a simple glance through a peephole three inches wide and two inches thick." He added dryly, "All of Vilenov's guards, by the way, were screened and verified to have never before come into contact with the prisoner. If our man, through some unknowable process, *is* able to produce a weird hold on people, we want to make sure the ones around him are untainted, so to speak." Prentis lifted his glasses symbolically and gave Abram a deep, meaningful wink. "Just to keep the queasy at ease. Anyways, cell cameras show the guard opening the door and letting Vilenov out. Corridor cameras follow them casually making their way. At each gate an officer buzzes the lock and ushers them through. This goes on all the way to Property, with a growing cast of uniforms escorting Vilenov like royalty.

"The guards go back to their stations, and Vilenov begins badgering the Property officer like an eager shopper. After rooting through the entire room, the officer finally comes up with a complete zoot suit, if you can believe it, crazy brim and all. Vilenov puts the suit on and does a little soft-shoe for the camera, then pulls the hat low over his face and sashays out of there. Exit the Houdini-rapist. The suit was found hanging half out of a garbage bin two hours later. But no sign of Vilenov. Police hit the area immediately and with intensity. Dozens of people report seeing a logy guy tripping down the sidewalk in a zoot suit, snapping his fingers and singing, 'Livin' la Vida Loca.' In the last sighting he was dancing outside a sporting goods store while staring in the window. The store's manager was hauled out of bed by police and questioned. No recollection of Vilenov. The manager was then dragged back to his store for inventory. It seems likely Vilenov changed his disguise with articles from the store. This got to be really tacky. Every employee had to be rousted during the wee hours to account for articles present and missing. A salesgirl and a cashier got antsy and refused to cooperate; it's pretty obvious they'd been ripping from the store. Oh, it'll all get sorted out, but by that time Vilenov will certainly have altered his whole appearance."

Prentis chomped a cherry and took a long swallow of his drink. "One of the first things to come out of this is that the floor safe was robbed of several thousand dollars. The manager was the only one present with access to the safe's combination. So then of course *he* gets defensive. The store's owner, who handles another outlet in Phoenix, is contacted. Accusations start flying all over the place. Police at the store treat the whole thing like a domestic situation, while detectives struggle over inventory. Precious time is lost. Vilenov could have hopped a bus to Long Beach, and from there a cab to San Diego. By now he could be happily bopping señoras in sunny Mazatlan."

Abram groaned.

After a minute the DA said, "Larry, there are elements to this case that go way beyond the unusual."

"That's pretty astute, Nelson," Abram grated. "I salute your acumen." He downed half his drink in a swallow.

Prentis nodded, said, "Now for the bad news," and turned to stare at a fenced-off space below, where a massive

crow was scattering sparrows in a widespread carpet of crois-
sant crumbs. "First off," he said, swirling a hand languidly,
"let's look at Marilyn Purly's apartment complex, where Mr.
Fred Mars, that holdout tenant on the petition Scarboro circu-
lated, for some inexplicable reason decides to take a header off
the landing outside his door at one-fifteen this morning. Cracks
his skull wide open on the drive and dies instantly. Nobody sees
a thing, of course, and nobody has a clue. Now let's look at an
ugly event, apparently unrelated and of far greater interest, that
takes place miles away but only minutes later." Prentis slowly
swiveled his gaze until he was looking directly into the black
lenses masking Abram's eyes. "Doctor Edward Karl Reis was
found dead by his own hand at one twenty-five this morning.
Both legally and literally." A shudder rolled across the table and
up Prentis's reclining arm. "And Larry, he sure didn't go gently
into that good night. According to the coroner's initial report,
Reis attempted to strangle himself, using both hands, leaving
two very deep handprints with matching bruises on the thumbs
and fingers. This was not a rational attempt at suicide, my
friend. It was done in wild rage by a man completely out of his
mind. I've never heard of such a case, except for one self-abort-
ed attempt maybe five years ago, by some nut on angel dust.
The good doctor, by the way, had nothing more toxic in his
system than the remains of a double cappuccino. Obviously this
kind of suicide can't be done. The worst you can do is make
yourself black out, which is what the coroner figures happened.

"The next indication is that he came to his senses and
tried to garrote himself with one of his ties, then with a lamp
cord. These were very intense acts, Larry, resulting in a sham-
bles for twenty square feet. They didn't work either, for the
same reason. Corresponding abrasions on the knuckles and face
demonstrate that the man actually tried to punch himself to
death with his own fists. But finally he got down on his hands
and knees and butted his head against the front door jamb until
he knocked himself into a coma. He died of a brain hemorrhage
on the way to the hospital. A herd of neighbors responded to the
ruckus with almost simultaneous 911 calls. Not a soul can ver-
ify a visitor to the doctor's home; no one saw anything other
than the usual skateboarders and news vans and some guy rid-

ing by in his exercise sweats. The house has been cordoned and the local Neighborhood Watch interviewed. The whole street's freaked out. So far the investigation shows not a scrap, not a hint, not a ghost of an intruder."

"Look, Nelson, lock me in a bank vault, okay? Surround me with Secret Service agents and attack dogs. Put me somewhere he can't find me. *Think of something!*" He tore at his drink. "Help me out, Nellie!"

Prentis swirled the ice in his glass. "Oh, if I were you I wouldn't get started on the funeral arrangements just yet. All the stops are being pulled on this case. The manhunt's already under way, with the Police Chief's and Mayor's support, and a boatload of promises from the governor. Vilenov will be so busy running he won't have a moment to rest, much less dwell on past slights." He shifted in his seat. "But for all that, how do you suppose he'd get his hands on you, anyway? All you have to do is keep moving. Don't hang out where he expects to find you."

"He didn't get his hands on Reis, or on Beasely—or on Frederick Mars or Marilyn Purly for that matter."

Prentis looked at him sharply. "Now wait a minute, buddy. What you're suggesting is paranormal activity, and that's a lot of silly crap to take seriously in the 21st century. Maybe you'd better taper off on the happy water. It sure ain't making you happy." He lost himself in an elongated drum roll. The drumming ceased abruptly. "Look, I'm not saying you don't have a right to be concerned, but you've got no call to go over the deep end, intellectually speaking."

"There are four gruesome deaths, Nelson, and this asshole had a score to settle, valid or otherwise, with each individual. I *know*. He told me things you wouldn't believe."

"And you would? Jesus. Listen, man, there are two suicides, a fall, and a tragic, very messy homicide, and in each case Vilenov was either restrained or manifestly nowhere near the premises." He rolled his shoulders. "I hate to say it, but if anybody's got alibis, it's him. Now, c'mon, Larry, I don't like him either. He gives me the willies, and I'd sleep a whole lot easier knowing he was history. But he's no demon, and he's no lunatic. Don't give him that much credit. He's just another filthy pervert, but one with a knack for getting out of jams." Prentis took a deep breath and rubbed his eyes, ran a hand through his stiff graying hair. "Your attitude is totally symptomatic of what this whole manhunt's about. Technically, the guy's done nothing worse than escape from confinement twice. His first walk was officially cleared by the L.A. verdict. The second time he was in protective confinement, and only because of a panicky call to the mayor. But nobody really gives a damn about any of that anymore. The public's freaked out, my boss is pissed, and there's *not* going to be a third time! So just relax, already. We've got a two-part plan. Part One is to put the lid on what could become a countywide panic by convincing the public we're right on him. Part Two is to snag the son of a bitch. And when we get him we're gonna lock him in a dark room before we work out a way to deport him. There are a lot of places in the Middle East I wouldn't mind seeing this guy dumped. Let them worry about him for a while." He smiled coldly. "This is going to come out fine. There won't be any more of his stunts. And no more shoddy police work."

"And then what?"

"And then you and the rest of the girls can fan yourselves and put away your tea leaves and Ouija boards. You can reopen your windows and get on with your lives. And *you personally*, my friend, can ease off the firewater and return to your practice like a proud, civilized man."

Abram again shook his head.

Prentis copied the movement with a practiced sarcasm that quickly deteriorated to genuine sympathy. He self-consciously cupped Abram's hand in his own. "Listen, Larry, why don't you and the family head on up to Big Bear? Make it four trips this year. There's every reason to believe he'll be coming back here; to Venice or to the Marina." Abram drew his hand away, and Prentis's demeanor instantly became businesslike. "You know as well as I that this area, on a late summer weekend, will be absolutely unmanageable. So the manhunt'll emphasize subtlety. Rather than a concrete police presence, there'll be a huge force of undercover spotters. The Venice circus this very morning acquired eighty-seven new members; everything from retirees, to security, to coast and fire. I've never seen such a surge of volunteerism." He eyeballed the sedate marina. "Look around you, Larry. As pleasant as pleasant can be. Men all over the county are sending families to distant relatives, or locking 'em indoors. Women are dressing down and wearing veils. But not in the Venice-Marina area; not in the one place everyone expects him to show. Here guys are sporting those stupid glasses with the decals of Vilenov's eyes on the lenses, and women are wearing the see-through DO ME, NICKY! blouses. This kind of crap is selling like crazy right out on the strand. Vilenov is pure camp. And he'll be here, trying to fit right back in. I can feel it in my bones. But we're ready, Larry. Every house he's familiar with is back under surveillance, and all plain-clothes officers are ordered to stun on sight. Volunteers have received a crash course in the use of pepper spray, with directions to spray first and ask questions later."

"I can see it now," Abram moaned. "Courtrooms full of weirdos in Vilenov glasses who've been pepper-sprayed by meter maids disguised as fortune tellers and massage therapists."

Prentis frowned wryly. "Was that the sound of you licking your lips, old buddy? Don't worry. There'll be plenty of time to deal with sunshine lawsuits later. Nothing's gonna come down in court. Besides, from every indication you've given me, you're not particularly interested in sticking around for the Vilenov feeding frenzy."

Abram shook his head gloomily. He squirmed a bit in his chair, tilted his head side to side. He seemed to be having trouble swallowing. Suddenly his tongue was protruding and his dark glasses hanging half off his face. Abram tore at his collar and snapped back his head.

The next thing Prentis knew he was standing behind his friend with his hands clasped below the breastbone, halfway into the Heimlich maneuver. Abram shook him off. Prentis waved away a few customers crossing the deck and returned to his seat.

Abram coughed wretchedly, picked up his hat and shoved his shades on tight. "I'm cool."

"That does it. I want you to lay off drinking for a while, man. You're a bundle of nerves, and the alcohol isn't helping a bit. You're just too high-strung."

"It wasn't the rum. I felt like I was on the gallows for a minute there." Abram's nails scratched across the glass table-top. "Nelson, I'm begging you, as a personal friend and as a caring human being: find a way to get me and mine back together and out of town!"

"Slow down!"

But Abram plowed right ahead. "Big Bear sounds like just the ticket. Later, after this is all over and Vilenov's history, I'll come back and you can have a good long laugh at my gullibility. I won't complain." He faced the Marina substation, almost a mile away. "Nelson, I know something you don't. Ever since the first time I interviewed the guy, in that sheriff's station over there, something really heavy's been going on in the back of my head. I can't explain it in plain terms—you'd only call it nerves and rum-reason. So I won't bother trying. I'll just tell you I fully empathize with everybody who's come into contact with that maniac." He lifted his shades to expose the sincerity in his eyes. "He's *here*, man! You talk about feeling it in your bones! My Vilenov radar is screaming at me, Nellie!"

"Fine. Then he's as good as in the bag."

Abram killed his drink. His next words amounted to an ultimatum. "Get me and my family out of town for a while. That's all. So help me, Nelson, I'll never ask you for another thing so long as I live."

Prentis pushed himself to his feet. "Okay, let's go. We'll grab a cab and you can stay at my place for now. I've *really* got to get back to the office. As soon as I can make time I'll get on the horn to Babs. You know she'll listen to me. I'll reconnect you two. Then I'm going to sleep the sleep of the dead. But you've got to promise me something. *Promise* me you'll apologize to her, from the heart, for being such a jerk. You're a luckier man than you'll ever realize."

"I know it!" Abram moaned. "God *knows* I know it!" He licked his lips, pulled the Homburg's brim lower over his shades. "One thing first. Just order us another round."

The DA took his arm. "I've got to get back, Larry."

"Then we'll get 'em to go."

"Come *on*." Prentis placed a Hamilton under his empty glass. He prodded his friend along with an occasional shove at the small of the back, smiling at customers and staff all the way.

Chapter Nine

The Flight

Finding the home address of Dr. Edward Karl Reis was a piece of cake. Anyone walking into that courtroom walked out a celebrity, and so became a member of the video-bite carousel. After reviewing the same old clip of a harassed-looking Reis being escorted to his Ladera Heights home, Vilenov located his address in the phone book and made for the area. He was well disguised.

On entering the sporting goods outlet he'd immediately influenced the manager. That was at nine p.m. At ten o'clock he exited walking a top-flight European mountain bike, with over six thousand dollars stuffed in his fancy extra large backpack. Also in the backpack were a change of clothes, five pounds of trail mix, and the largest, deadliest hunting knife the manager could find. Vilenov was wearing an oversized green rayon parka, baggy gray exercise pants, and heavy leather hiking boots. The outfit altogether altered his appearance; he was no longer the grooving sidewalk peacock, nor the instantly recognizable gnarly fugitive. The parka billowed as he moved, its fur-fringed hood hiding all but his nose and chin. The sweatpants and boots made him a clunky, shapeless silhouette in a hectic world of blinding headlights and lancing neon. It may have seemed a strange outfit for a lovely September evening, but this was Los Angeles, where the unordinary was ordinary. Vilenov switched on the headlight of his brand new 21-speed mountain bike and pushed off down the sidewalk.

Ladera Heights is an upscale community on the outskirts of Inglewood, only a few miles from the ocean and not completely unfamiliar to a man who'd spent most of his life in Venice Beach. It was a long ride from Downtown L.A., but Vilenov wasn't in a hurry. Though news of his escape blared from every car radio, he purposefully avoided shadows, emboldened by the tension. He grinned maniacally at pedestrians, ran red lights, darted through traffic—and all this non-paranoiac behavior made him look that much less suspicious. Beginning to enjoy the ride, he casually tapped the huge hunting knife on the handlebars while fantasizing the meticulous skinning of Reis. The blade was a good one; it would surely retain the bite to complete, by tomorrow at the latest, the drawn-out disemboweling of a certain duplicitous, rip-off defense attorney.

It was coming up on midnight when he rolled down La Brea into Inglewood. Streets were dark and quiet, the sky aching with stars. Vilenov, cockier by the mile, purchased a six-pack of Heinekens at a corner convenience store, chugged four bottles in the parking lot, and smashed the remainder on the asphalt. Aggressively drunk, he jammed the bike to Centinela while still riding the initial rush. In less than ten minutes he was zigzagging through Ladera Heights. Vilenov peed like a race horse behind a van, found the street he wanted, and pushed his bike uphill. Soon he was teetering on the lip of the curb opposite Reis's house.

He dropped his bike and backpack on the sidewalk, pulled the knife from under his parka, and marched straight across the street. But the instant his foot met the property's walk he was illuminated by porch floods flanking a wall-mounted security camera. A variety of alarms were activated on Reis's gold Mercedes, cueing an enormous mastiff in the doctor's backyard. The whole neighborhood came alive with howling sentinels. Lights burned in the houses to either side. Drapes were drawn aside.

"*Jee*-sus!" Vilenov tiptoed back to his bike as the facing houses lit up like Christmas trees. By the time he'd shrugged on his backpack and straddled his machine the street was a blinding, wailing madhouse. Vilenov coasted down the sidewalk crazily, veering on and off of lawns, into and out of the street. The front door of each passed house blew open to eject a sputtering homeowner, as though triggered by the friction of his spinning wheels. A pair of private security vehicles whipped around the corner. Half a minute later sirens were approaching fast on Centinela.

Vilenov kept right on riding, wobbling away from everything in his path, and by the time he pulled into the Mini Mart on La Cienega he was rattled, paranoid, and pissed. He took a nervous leak behind the trash bin, stormed inside and bought two quart bottles of Colt .45 malt liquor. Vilenov crammed one in his backpack, tore the cap off the other, and coasted down La Cienega toward the freeway. He had to walk the bike where the boulevard arched uphill. Having paused halfway to chug the quart in thirds, Vilenov accurately hurled the drained bottle at a parked car's windshield. Upon reaching the tracks just north of Florence, he remounted, veered left through traffic, and pitched headfirst over the curb into pebbles and scrub. Vilenov came up spitting blood, out of his mind with rage and alcohol.

The 405 overpass at Florence includes a wide swath of crushed rock to accommodate tracks and ties. This left Vilenov plenty of room to stagger about unmolested until he reached the steel and cement rail overlooking the lanes some thirty feet below. He caught the rail at his waist and clung there, doubled over, staring deliriously at tons of hurtling metal. He wanted to heave but didn't dare, wanted to haul himself back up but couldn't move a muscle. The dazzling succession of sweeping headlights threw his mind into a magic lantern parade of memorized exploits. Lovers and enemies flickered and passed; each one a galling memory and slap to his pride. A whipped, stupefied gargoyle, Vilenov hung there snarling and slavering, paralyzed. And the freeway became a familiar driveway, and the rail at his waist became the rail on the upper landing opposite the apartment of that double-crossing bitch of a girlfriend. He was leaning on this rail tensely, staring at some frail old black man standing right beside him. The man was watching him hard. Moreover, he knew that this old man had something on him, and had to be mollified. But now Vilenov, visualizing himself

paranoically kissing up to that devious prying rat, became absolutely livid with rage. In his imagination he hurled the filthy old
snoop over the rail onto his cracking black busybody skull, then
almost fainted from the resulting pain in his own head. His
backpack had him; his center of gravity was between his shoulder blades...was at the back of his neck, was at his crown...he
was about to be mangled and mashed into psycho jam, dragged
flopping-all-fours through the rocketing madness below. He had
to recover...had to push back...he had to right himself, or he'd
be smeared, from here to San Pedro, by ten thousand rushing
wheels.

An old nightmare, common to dreamers, returned to
claim him. He was on his stomach on a tall building's roof, his
fingers numbly clenching the edge while the building gradually
tilted. Nerveless and helpless, unable to feel his thighs or toes,
he could only slip with the building until he was launched toward the yawning vortex below. Yet even as he was falling Vilenov was able to shove himself back from the abyss and onto
the cotton-soft bed of jumbled rocks behind him. He rocked and
rolled to his feet, grabbed his bicycle and ran weaving back to
La Cienega. Halfway across the street his foot was tangled in
spokes. He sprawled face-first on top of his bicycle, kicking and
flailing his arms in the midst of braking and honking vehicles.
Clinging to the handlebars, Vilenov found his feet and continued stumbling across traffic, flipping off drivers as he went.

Back on the west side of La Cienega, he rammed his
bike between the tracks, shoved it over the ties for a quarter
mile, and collapsed in the dirt near Florence and Manchester.
He struggled to his knees. On the incline between the tracks and
bordering bushes he tore off the puppet master of his backpack,
crushed it in a bear hug and punched its lights out until his fists
rang on glass. Vilenov pulled out the remaining quart of Colt
and attempted to chug it, but the brew blew out his nostrils.
Fighting for breath and hyperventilating, he forced the contents
down, smashed the bottle on a rail, and brought the glass neck
back in a handful of blood.

Nicolas Vilenov pivoted on his knees until he was facing the bushes. Embracing his stomach, he lowered his head almost to the ground, arched his spine, and puked his guts out. A

minute later he clawed back up the incline with the disembodied face of Edward Reis hovering before him like a bone-white balloon, mocking his lunges, jerking away in little spurts that perfectly matched his lurching progress. Vilenov, swinging wildly, followed it onto the tracks, bashing his knuckles on the rails until his hands chanced upon a depleted fire extinguisher entangled in a yard of packing twine. Now the face of Reis appeared to float up out of the cylinder and stand on its surface like a sneering decal. Vilenov took the extinguisher in a stranglehold and squeezed till his hands could take no more, then tightly wrapped the trailing twine. He garroted the cylinder before bashing his bloody fists repeatedly against its smooth steel side.

The extinguisher rolled down the embankment with Vilenov furiously scrambling behind, straight into the bordering line of thorny, exhaust-dusted bushes. He swung and kicked wildly, tore at the parka's snagged hood, butted the branches with his face and skull. Backpedaling in a crouch, he pitched onto the ties and immediately went into seizure. Gradually the spasms diminished. Vilenov lay absolutely still, spread-eagled on the tracks and staring at the cold moon through pinched and streaming eyes; a catastrophe just waiting to happen.

That crazy bull elephant kept right on coming in slow motion, trumpeting over its own rhythmic background of gasps and grunts. Vilenov melted into the landscape, trying to breathe with the wind, trying to wave with the tall grass, doing everything he could to become one with the savanna. But the bull's beady black eyes were fixed on him. Its body enlarged tenfold with each bound, the phallic old trunk moving pendulously, swinging wider and higher as it neared. Vilenov couldn't run, couldn't rise, couldn't even react; his limbs were stuck in muck, and every part of his body was numb. Two more bounds and the monster made its final lunge. During that leap it seemed to float like a dirigible, eclipsing the desert panorama, the sun, the very sky—landing at last with one long blaring, all-obliterating *stomp*.

Vilenov screamed down the embankment as the train hammered by, stopping his ears against the angry drawn-out howl of its horn. Not until the caboose was a tiny receding box did he gingerly pick himself free of the filthy bushes and blown litter.

Both bike and backpack were covered with dirt and crawling with ants. They were badly tangled in the dense growth separating Florence Boulevard and the tracks. It was just after dawn. He spent some time nursing his injured hand and tongue, then shrugged on his backpack and, looking for all the world like a penniless tramp, pushed his bike alongside the tracks to Manchester, his parka and sweatpants in tatters, his face all scratches and scabs.

Vilenov coasted to the Burger King on Bellanca, stood his bike in the rack, and waited in line with his hooded head down. After furtively fishing a five from his backpack, he ordered breakfast and coffee in the hoarsest of whispers. Hanging around waiting with the rest of the customers drove him crazy, so he nonchalantly stepped outside and bought a Times with the change from his five.

There he was, all over the front page, immortalized in that notorious booking photo. Beside his banner image were three small photographs aligned vertically. Vilenov snarled.

Hatch.

Prentis.

Abram.

He slunk back inside, carried his paper and tray to the remotest table. Vilenov held the newspaper propped in front of his face with one hand while he picked at his food with the other.

Lots of confused tough-talk had preceded the morning edition, resulting in an uneven battle plan designed to leave the masses with the impression that things were perfectly under control.

But right before that the state must have gone mad.

After an intensely uncomfortable wee hours confab with the mayor, the governor had agreed to place troops of the National Guard on standby. L.A.'s Chief of Police, during a bizarre three a.m. news conference in a packed West L.A. cathedral, had followed with the announcement of a countywide manhunt. Citizens were warned to avoid strangers. Vilenov was described as desperate, dangerous, and all but apprehended. Long before sunrise, day care centers, playgrounds, and elementary schools were hiring armed security guards. Vilenov frowned. Why did these people insist on treating him as a pedophile? He read on. Overnight, Hollywood had become *the* source for Vilenov sightings. Barely twelve hours on the street, and he was already responsible for the rapes of nineteen runaways and over thirty prostitutes.

Police in the beach communities of Venice and Santa Monica detained one hundred and ninety-three destitute men during that early morning scramble. Naturally, the area's homeless advocates were instantly up in arms; blocking streets and courthouses in anticipation of the morning rush. But not all veteran residents of Venice-Santa Monica were upset with the new ultra-heavy police presence; decent people all around thrilled as crack whores, border hoppers, shopping cart squatters, street preachers, and all manner of UFO *abductees* abandoned the area en masse. A quote from Reis made Vilenov bristle:

> *"This man, still haunted by pubescent fantasies, will flee to the one place he believes will have him; he will run home. But it would be unwise to view this as merely an instinctive attempt to evade his pursuers. Mr. Vilenov* needs *to be pursued. He needs the rush."*

Vilenov squeezed his fists under the table, and just like that a huge wall mirror across the room burst into a hundred pieces, the shards ringing on tabletops and floor. Every face in the place watched mesmerized as he dumped his tray in a trash container and stormed from the building.

His cool new bicycle was long gone. Vilenov closed his eyes and lowered his head. It took a hefty session of controlled deep breathing, but he managed to compose himself. He shrugged his backpack tighter and tramped west on Manchester, grudgingly admitting Reis was right: even an animal knows enough to turn home. White light crackled in his skull.

And Vilenov was sitting in a slump on a cement bench, staring at nothing.

His entire face was masked in sweat; he could feel it seeping out of his matted hair under the parka's hood. With an effort he closed his gaping mouth and brought his eyes back into focus. When a city bus pulled up five minutes later he boarded self-consciously and inserted a dollar in the slot. Not a face turned as he passed, but every eye watched him walk unsteadily down the aisle and squeeze beside a pregnant Latina. The bus was packed. Vilenov, peeping groggily from beneath his parka's drawn hood, saw a split field of barely averted faces. He put his hands in the parka's pockets and lowered his head as though snoozing. After a couple miles of this the dull ache in his temple grew to a screaming pain. Vilenov's jaws clamped shut, his head rocked back, his eyes rolled up. He looked like a man being electrocuted. The faces lining the aisle slowly turned in unison. Their eyes coldly watched him sitting bolt-upright, his Adam's apple thrust out, his white fingers tearing into his knees. Except for the muffled sounds of traffic and the engine's steady hum, the world inside the bus was dead-quiet. Finally a long rasping breath escaped between Vilenov's teeth. His chin dropped to his chest. Pink flecks shifted rapidly at the corners of his mouth while the light fluttered in and out of his dull gray eyes. His hands relaxed and the faces just as slowly turned away. With tears covering his cheeks, Vilenov struggled to his feet, slammed against a seat, and staggered down the aisle between the quickly turning pairs of knees. He grabbed the vertical pole by the front steps and the weight of his backpack almost propelled him onto his rear. The driver wordlessly pulled to the curb at Lincoln Boulevard. The doors hissed open and Vilenov pitched out, straight through the open front doorway of the corner liquor store. He watched from behind the store's display window as the bus passed the next bench without pausing.

Vilenov bought a bag of beef jerky, a half pint of vodka, and a 16-ounce can of Old English malt liquor for a chaser. The in-store television showed the mayor addressing a news conference; assuring the good citizens of L.A. that, although time was running out for Nicolas Vilenov, he was still considered extremely dangerous. The mayor introduced a Colonel Peebles, liaison officer for police and National Guard. Peebles warned civilians to prepare for the sight of military vehicles on their generally quiet streets.

The clerk, a round Nicaraguan with a Raiders cap and caterpillar moustache, slapped his palm on the counter. "Look like they just about get that guy, eh, amigo?" Vilenov lowered his head. "What you think about that spooky stuff? Eh? You think he bite woman? You think he do little children?" The clerk, uncertain of Vilenov's race, seemed to be making a game of trying to get a peek at his face. "¿Niños?" he said.

"I dunno," Vilenov grunted. "Nowadays I can believe just about anything."

"You right!" The clerk slapped the counter again. "People today got no Jesus!"

"I'm hip to that," Vilenov whispered. "Thanks, dude."

"You drink him down, man. Kill cold in no time. And when you done you come back for more."

"Viva la whatever," Vilenov rasped. As soon as he hit the sidewalk he threw away the beef jerky and split the cap on the vodka. The first swallow obliterated his sense of persecution, the second did wonders for his headache.

It was a long walk down Lincoln to Venice. Halfway there Vilenov's half-pint was history, the malt liquor merely backwash. He decided to take a chance at the Marina Market on Mindanao Way, prudently buying a fifth this time to save himself the risk of another trip. The whole place was uptight. The liquor clerk didn't say a word, but took Vilenov's money and slapped down the change.

Vilenov stepped outside and gazed over the Marina. Before him was the market's parking lot, then the thin asphalt curve of Admiralty Way. Across Admiralty stretched a bike path and, beyond, a low fence surrounding the harbor's launch ramps, where hundreds of sails poked up like bleached stalagmites. Vilenov zigzagged between the parked cars to Admiralty and dashed across the road at the first break in traffic. The pretty little bike path was, as always, a liquid parade of tobogganing bicyclists, pimp-walking roller skaters, and obscenely spandexed hausfrau in ponytails and sports bras.

He sat heavily on a wood bench in a cloud of gulls, regretting not having picked up a loaf to toss, slice by precious slice. It was already warm, but he remained bundled in the parka. Vilenov broke the cap on the vodka, took a long swallow. Fiji Way, to his left, ran west to Fisherman's Village, a collection of gift shops looking over South Channel. In the cul-de-sac of Fiji was the Marina del Rey Sheriff's substation, his first stop after the Purly raid. To his right was Mindanao, a short road terminating in the small artificial peninsula of Chace Park. Vilenov took another swallow. For no reason at all Abram's face came to him, drifting into his mind more like an afterthought than a memory. Vilenov's free hand clenched once, twice. The squeezing motion felt good, as if that self-serving pig was close enough to squeal. He tilted back the bottle, and the alcohol was like acid on his lips and tongue. He had to squint to see. The area was so picturesque it was hard to imagine such a thing as a manhunt. The air was very sweet and clear.

When he woke it was late afternoon. He was on his side with his knees drawn up and his hands tucked between his thighs; just another Venice derelict on the wrong side of the tracks. His backpack was gone. Vilenov rolled off his bench and staggered to the Marina's information center, a quaint little nautical cottage at the corner of Mindanao and Admiralty. Mercifully, the restroom door was unlocked. He splashed water on his face and hair, paid his respects to the urinal, and turned around completely unprepared for the bloody ragged creature in the mirror. Vilenov tore off the parka and screamed until the pain in his head made him cling desperately to the sink. A minute later he yanked open the door and went stumbling north along the bike path with venom in his eyes. Bicyclists, fighting their machines, rode well around him, joggers stopped to look back with strange expressions. On all sides, strollers turned angrily or fearfully, lovers' hands unlocked and clenched into fists. Tiny pockets of rubbernecks grew, uncertain of their emotions.

Vilenov stomped across the street to that long swath of shaved grass opposite Sweet Harbor known as Admiralty Park. Here the bike path, crossing Admiralty Way at an abrupt signal, continues along in a two-lane bisection of this swath, curving gently between exercise stations and dog walks. Vilenov stormed past sunbathers, sightseers, and assorted loitering chatterbrains, past dippers and danglers and dealers, tromping along furiously until a high trio of helicopters caught his attention. He watched very narrowly for a minute, trying to find a pattern. When he looked back down black-and-whites were all over the place. He instinctively joined the crowd, and as he worked his way into the thickest part of the packed park things quickly went from sociable to surreal. All around were opposing tables of Hysterics and Enablers, enlisting the audience of gaping crackheads and vagabonds while Jesus freaks worked hard to convert insolent Vilenov freaks. Riot-helmeted bicycle cops in short pants and white polo shirts gingerly coasted throughout the little park, back and forth across Admiralty, up and down the neighboring street. All sense of sobriety, of basic sanity, and of social etiquette, had absolutely gone to Hell. He smiled and relaxed. He was nearing Venice.

There was a hard squeal of tires. Vilenov raised himself on his toes to see a sheriff's car neatly cutting off the park's entrance. He lowered his face and pushed his way back to the bike path.

Waiting at the park's far end, a pair of those roving sentinels stood straddling their bikes' frames, admitting exit and egress like nightclub bouncers. Vilenov's only course was obvious. He tied his shirt around his neck, stuck a stupid look on his face, and began to jog, smothering his features as he chugged between the coldly watching pillars. Following the bike path down, he came puffing upon Washington Boulevard and almost sagged with relief.

He was home.

The ocean was less than a mile to his left, and just north of the Admiralty-Washington intersection were the Venice Canals. And *everywhere* were black-and-whites; their noses poking out of subterranean garages, their roof lights standing out amidst parked cars. Helicopters, aggressively monitoring the Venice Beach crowd, were swarming over the strand like flies over a dog's mess.

Vilenov nonchalantly fell in with a small herd jogging in place at the corner. When the light changed he panted along to the far curb, but as the others turned and flapped gasping to the beach he made a hard right and jiggled up to Laguna Liquor on the corner of Washington and Abbot Kinney. He jogged straight into the store and fixed the clerk with his cold gray eyes. The man dutifully bagged all the register's twenties with a pint of sloe gin while Vilenov ran in place, studying the shelves. A few seconds later the clerk turned. With the nervous delicacy of a man handling eggs, he stacked on the counter: a pair of fancy iridescent inline roller skates, an AC/DC baseball cap with built-in radio and headphones, bright blue wraparound sunglasses, and a red and white bandana. Vilenov nodded, scooped up the stack, and jogged back outside. Still hopping foot to foot, he stuffed the bills in his underwear, tied the bandana round his forehead, found a hard-rock station, and slapped the cap on backward. He sat on the curb to catch his breath, yanked off his boots, tied the laces together, looped the boots around his neck. Vilenov then laced on the skates and awkwardly pushed himself upright. He placed the gaudy shades over his eyes and studied his reflection in a plate glass window. Not bad. A few tattoos and nose rings, a pair of leopard skin bikini shorts, and he'd be Venice-all-over. He guzzled two thirds of the pint, reeled a ways on his new skates, and smashed the remainder on the sidewalk. Sloe gin is tough on the plumbing.

Vilenov clumsily skated Washington east, pushing off parked cars to maintain his balance. By the time he'd reached Lincoln Boulevard the sun was fuzzying the horizon.

Lincoln was filthy with cops, up and down; plainclothes loitering at the bus stops, bicycle patrollers on every corner. Emboldened by alcohol, Vilenov skated awkwardly across the intersection, falling twice. A bicycle cop helped him up and warned him to be careful: he was in a heavily monitored, officially-sanctioned search area. Vilenov, rubbing a skinned knee, thanked him effusively. He certainly didn't want to run into any nasty criminals. Directly overhead, a helicopter dipped, rose, and veered south. Vilenov skated on for a block before rolling straight into a vacant wrought iron bench. He tore off the skates and cap and dropped them in a trash can, laced on his boots and tottered into the new mall's supermarket. There he bought a 750 milliliter bottle of Hiram Walker's excellent apricot brandy. Vilenov cussed out a pair of stupid dawdling old

118

ladies, scattered a train of stupid useless shopping carts, and went staggering through the parking lot gulping sweet fire.

In the deepening blue Nicolas Vilenov began to feel wonderful; lightheaded, strong, independent. It wasn't just the brandy. It was a combination of freedom, gorgeous weather, and all those recent encounters that had worked in his favor. He was feeling very full of himself. The state's most recognizable man was able to boldly blunder behind enemy lines and come out smelling like a rose.

An LAPD cruiser passed slowly, even as he was insolently raising the brandy to his lips. Vilenov defiantly tore off his shades and flung them aside. *C'mon, man*, he thought, *bust me!* The car moved along, and Vilenov's little burst of passion passed as quickly as it had come. He took another swallow and went weaving between the parked cars, having never felt so unfettered, so unhurried, so indifferent to the big picture. It was like being in some goofy Broadway musical, where the innocent young hero wanders about on the wings of love, unaware of staring passersby.

But he wasn't in love—few men in the world were as far removed from that priceless state as Nicolas Vilenov. So maybe this crazy feeling was just trying to tell him he was ready. Maybe his new love was right here, in this very parking lot, and maybe their eyes would simply *lock.* Just like in some goofy Broadway musical. He gulped the brandy and licked his lips. She wouldn't have to be gorgeous, of course. She'd just have to be nice, and vulnerable, and stacked to the rafters. He smiled at the women walking by.

No, not her.

And no, not her.

Or her.

But then he saw heaven from behind, bending over to scooch shopping bags on the back seat of a dark green Accord. Oh yes. Shoulder-length brown hair and pretty little kitty face. Beige leggings and tight fuzzy sweater. All the good, all the important parts screaming against the material. Just begging for it.

As she swung shut the door he sauntered over and looked her straight in her pretty brown eyes, gave her his widest smile, and let his gaze run up and down her ripe-to-bursting body. Still riding his Broadway fantasy, Vilenov bowed deeply and said with all the gallantry he could muster,

"Hi! My name's Nicolas. But you can just call me Nicky. That's what all my bitches call me. We'll be going for a drive now, and then I think we might have a bite and take in a little TV before bed. Don't worry. I'm absolutely sure you're going to like me." He stepped around to the passenger side and waited for her to unlock his door, a dreamy tune in his head. As she backed out the car he took another long swallow. "I'd be glad to share some of this with you, m'dear, but the cops in this town are really down on drinking and driving. Every day I thank the good Lord they're out there, sniffing and testing, citing and towing, keeping the public safe and sound." He carefully chugged a quarter of the remaining brandy, taking it down with little fish-like partings of the lips. His tongue was on fire. "What's your name?"

"Cindy. Cindy Mathe—"

"Cindy's just fine. Cindy, you and I are lovers. And tonight, baby, we're gonna hammer down the wind."

"Where…where are we going?" Her voice sounded tiny and robotic, like a round-hipped, skinny-waisted, big-busted talking doll for sweet little girls with long blonde braids.

Perfect.

"Oh…I don't know," he said breezily. "Why don't we just head west. I've always been partial to the beach."

Chapter Ten

The Influence

The Dunerider Hotel on Ocean Avenue features a breathtaking panorama of Venice Beach and the Pacific, a view made all the more enchanting by a killer sunset in a cloudless sky. Set in a wide wrought iron archway inlaid with polished turquoise, a cursive neon vacancy sign offers *CABLE* and *SATELLITE* and *FRESH SEAFOOD DINING*. It's no flophouse. When head of security saw the familiar-looking man approach the main desk escorting a lovely, distant young woman, a thousand bells went off in his naturally suspicious mind. But when the newcomer caught him in those pale gray eyes he was immediately inspired to shut down all security cameras and erase their tapes. He vanished through a small back door hidden by potted dwarf palms.

The desk clerk's eyes were on his ledger. Vilenov leaned tipsily against the desk and smiled warmly. "Your finest room, my man, with all the goodies."

The clerk's eyes, slithering across the desk, went foggy at the contents of the straining fuzzy sweater. His voice caught in his throat.

"Your wife?"

"You bet."

He looked enviously into the face of the hotel's newest customer. That envy was instantly removed from his expression, as though he'd been slapped. Every aspect of his tone and manner became respectfully businesslike.

"Will you be staying long, sir?"

"Just the night."

"Fine. I'll need to see some identification, please."

Vilenov grunted and thrust the brandy bottle under the man's nose so that his eyes were fixed on the label. The clerk dutifully scribbled in his ledger, saying, "Thank you, Mr. Walker." He reached below the counter to extract a single key on a ring. "I'm giving you number 4, our best available room. It's downstairs, and has a rear balcony with a stunning ocean view. In the room you will find a menu, a wide-screen TV with cable and satellite, and a brochure describing all our amenities and how you may access them with a simple phone call. If there's anything you need, or if you find anything unsatisfactory in any way, please just ring the desk and ask for the manager. Now, will you be paying in cash or by credit card?"

"Whatever," Vilenov said.

"Excellent. If you'll just sign the register, then."

Vilenov, leaning heavily on the desk, signed clumsily:

Hiram Walker

He pinched the bottle's neck with one hand and plucked the key from the clerk's fingers with the other, killed the brandy and tossed the empty bottle on the ledger. "You can start your room service with another one of these. And bring some ice, and some fresh underthings for the lady. And after that stay the hell away from my door."

It was late afternoon when he surfaced from a nightmare of rampaging pigs in jackboots. Never had he felt so sick. His head pounded as he rose, softened when he paused. Fighting to keep from vomiting, Vilenov forced himself to a sitting position little by little. He slid off the toppled, stained mattress, landing directly on his tailbone.

The room was a disaster. Liquor bottles, full and empty, lay scattered on the plush pile carpet. One curtain was half-torn from its rod. A wedge of sunlight tore at his eyes while he sat in a slump, nursing fractured memories of waking at dawn, of getting drunk again, of repeatedly assaulting the woman beside him with varying results. That was the rub of alcohol. Fires you up but lets you down.

He staggered into the bathroom, pitched back out and fumbled into his clothes, took two steps and collapsed on his knees. Cindy was supine; her face turned away, her fine brown hair spilt all around the pillow in a soft feathered fan. She couldn't have looked lovelier posing. Her breasts made the sheet a taut slope from nipples to thighs. He took a peek and shuddered. It was enough to make a man's man cry. She was a keeper, no question about it.

Vilenov had to walk on his knees to fix the curtain; if he'd tried to stand he would have passed right out. Halfway to the window he became aware of authoritative-sounding voices in the parking lot. He tentatively stuck his head into the wedge of light. What he saw sobered him instantly.

Five black-and-whites had control of the hotel's drive. Four others were barricading the street. Two units down, officers were moving door to door with guns drawn. At least three more were creeping through the parking lot, crouching and rising, peeking inside vehicles. Vilenov couldn't check himself: he slammed his fist into the wall.

Immediately one of the officers moving door to door went rigid, whirled, and threw a haymaker into the teeth of his partner. Within seconds there was a policeman's brawl in the parking lot. The first cop, swarmed by his buddies, went for his gun. Vilenov heard a shot. Then another. Tenants and staff ran screaming from the lobby while hunching pedestrians scattered behind anything stationary. In the confusion he stumbled into his boots, slipped outside, and ran zigzagging between cars. He hesitated, his temple pounding as hard as his heart. To his right, a picturesque cement staircase descended in sections street to street, terminating in a brief splash of cobblestones at Ocean Front Walk three flights below. Chain link separates this staircase from the Dunerider and adjacent property, but Vilenov couldn't afford to run clear up to the street and around, so he jumped on a car and vaulted the fence. No athlete, he tore his arm and trousers going over, then half ran, half rolled down the stairs to the promenade.

Ocean Front Walk, on a beautiful late summer's day, is an outrageous freak show all wound up with no place to go. Thousands of rowdy partygoers file along in rough ranks on a sidewalk two miles long and ten feet wide, occasionally obstructed by vendors, street musicians, and milling gangbangers. Vilenov was carried by the crowd; jostled by roller-skating blacks in Speedos, by glaring Latino furheads grudgingly comparing tattoos, by creepy white longhairs slinking across the walk to dig in ranks of fifty-five gallon trash drums. Sifting through all this were the camera-toting tourists, the beady-eyed skinheads, the glistening, overblown bodybuilders. Two helicopters appeared above the Dunerider. Another—sleek, black, and futuristic—tore south along the waterline at full tilt. Following with his eyes, Vilenov made out a number of distant police ATVs speeding his way over the sand. Closer by, lifeguards were clearing the beach of sunbathers. Vilenov pushed through the bodies, keeping low. Catching a break, he looked north to find Santa Monica Pier's paved boardwalk crawling with police cars. He was about to change direction when he heard the *whoop* of a siren behind him being triggered and released. The crowd ahead, whirling to see, instantly became an impenetrable human wall. Above their bobbing heads appeared the eggshell helmet of a mounted policeman.

The wall exploded the moment Vilenov panicked. A spike-haired youth beside him grabbed a man twice his size and went for his eyes. A pretty brown girl fell to her knees, screaming and tearing at her cheeks with her long purple nails. A table covered with specimens of Henna tattoos collapsed as if its legs had been kicked out. A homeless man knocked over the trash can he'd been dredging, then pursued the rolling can through the bewildered crowd, kicking and cursing all the way.

Now Vilenov, rammed from behind, turned to see the mêlée expanding like ripples in a pond. He staggered onto one of the little grass oases between the walk and adjacent serpentine bike path. The oasis was peppered by bicyclists dazed from collisions. Vilenov snatched the derailleur of a spandexed bicyclist sitting holding his gushing broken nose. The handlebars, wrenched left in the spill, wouldn't respond to his immediate attempts at adjustment, so he rode wobbling along the path towards the waterline, occasionally looking back.

The Ocean Front crowd, spilling onto the bike path and beach itself, was immediately corralled by dozens of plain-clothes officers leaping from behind kiosks and storefront countertops. Suddenly men with megaphones were everywhere. Vilenov saw ATVs making for the spot he'd just left, even as an unmarked car, its siren briefly howling every few seconds, lurched around frantic pedestrians. Before it had stopped completely a number of men jumped out and threw themselves into the shoving bodies, abandoning the car in the sand. Two sprinted into one of the many collapsible leased stores selling sunglasses and pop posters, chasing a man wearing a red bandana and baseball cap. Another helicopter appeared, this time very low over Ocean Front. The crowd went right into stampede mode.

He was breathing hard by the time he reached the short pier tunnel. Emerging cyclists, reacting to his anxiety, threw out their arms and pitched headfirst onto the asphalt path. Vilenov dropped his wheels. Clinging to the darkness, he crept like a spider to the bright world on the other side.

He poked out his head. Despite the very heavy police presence behind him, the beach on this side was still crowded, cut off from the sounds of panic.

Then sun worshippers were jumping up and plodding excitedly through the sand to Ocean Front. A knot of running pedestrians erupted into view. Seconds later a trio of police cars came pushing south from Ocean Front's far end, quickly overtaken by ATVs that leaped the road and tore across the sand. The slower sunbathers, looking around uncertainly, hollered questions, grabbed belongings, and scooped up errant toddlers.

Vilenov arched his shoulders and lowered his head. Melting out of the pier's shadow, he walked nonchalantly round a pillar and straight into a faceful of pepper spray.

He hit the ground with his hands clamped over his face; his eyes, sinuses, and throat on fire. Cayenne seared his lungs in brief, superheated bursts, remedied only by desperate little gulps of fresh ocean air. He thrashed about like a drowning man before pushing himself to his knees, his hot red face hanging beneath a high-pitched pumping noise. Vilenov wiped his streaming eyes and smacked his palms over his ears before that piercing, persistent screech could drill a hole right through the soft spot in his temple. Planted squarely in front of him, the offending blur swam into focus.

A squat, middle-aged woman in windbreaker and jogging sweats stood hunched with her fists on her hips, blowing frantically on a fat nickel-plated whistle. By alternately rubbing his eyes and rapidly blinking, Vilenov was able to make out the oval *Santa Monica Provisional Deputy* patch on the woman's black baseball cap, and the all-pervading anti-Vilenov image sewn into her windbreaker's breast.

"Gah!" he snarled, and she took off like a shot across the sand, still blowing her whistle maniacally. Not a soul paid her the least mind; every person on the beach was mesmerized by the human flash flood screaming down Ocean Front. Slapping his face and howling curses, Vilenov staggered to a drinking fountain, rinsed his mouth and spat, soaked his head, repeatedly splashed water in his eyes. His expression was startlingly feral as he bounded up the short flight of sand-to-boardwalk cement steps.

Almost every officer on the pier was caught up in the Ocean Front commotion; Vilenov watched them leaning over the promenade rail, running through the hangar-like arcade, circumnavigating the carousel—but one nervous patrolman was parked facing the water, maybe a hundred feet from the cement staircase. This officer's head popped out his window like a jack in the box, popped back inside. The cop stepped on the gas and made straight for him, their stares wed all the way. Suddenly the driver's eyes seemed to sizzle in his face. Gunning the engine, he planted his head squarely into his shoulders. The car accelerated past Vilenov to the very end of the pier, burst through the rail and made a picture-perfect swan dive into the sea.

The police overlooking the promenade whirled when they heard the cruiser's racing engine, then stood mesmerized as the car smashed into the wooden guardrail and appeared to hang suspended above the sea. Before it had vanished they were sprinting for the spot, the roar of their voices rolling up the boardwalk like a retreating wave. Vilenov took the steps back down three at a time. He stumbled through the sand to the Sidewalk Plaza, where pedestrians and customers greeted him with a rushing, shrieking free-for-all. He was battered and bitten, elbowed and kneed. Vilenov kicked and punched his way free while flags and sun umbrellas burst into flames around him. He scrambled crabwise up the embankment beneath the avenue-to-pier bridge.

Running under this bridge are the lanes connecting Pacific Coast Highway with the 10 freeway, and the onramp and offramp connecting PCH with Palisades Park, a famous clifftop swath with a breathtaking South Bay view. The two highway lanes lead into a short tunnel penetrating a low fat hillock at the cliff's foot, and emerge as diverging lanes which are, practically speaking, the westbound 10's terminus. Vilenov dashed across the ramps and paused on the dividing island to consider his three possible routes: he could dart in full sight across the highway to the base of the cliff, he could clamber up the tree-lined embankment over the tunnel until he reached the park, or he could sprint the few hundred yards through the tunnel out of view from above. Vilenov peered into the tunnel. That way was suicide. And a quick glance up revealed police cars moving off the bridge onto Pacific Avenue. No less than nine helicopters— police, news, and National Guard—were hovering about, a few positioned extremely high overhead. Hard to his left, a herd of black-and-whites were roaring up PCH. Without a moment to waste, he ran across the highway and began awkwardly making his way up the cliff's face, embracing one clump of brush before leaping to the next. There was a sudden ruckus from joggers and seniors leaning on the rail above, and some very aggressive barking from a police K9 unit. Down on the highway, a dozen CHP cars halted in ranks of three. On the beach beyond, eight south-running black and white ATVs met an equal number driving north. The vehicles parked in an odd arrangement that placed drivers facing in all directions, leaving a maze of tire tracks in the sand. Hard on his tail, a number of policemen were now kicking down homeless camps amid the stunted trees over the tunnel. A black helicopter came barreling north, halted above the ATVs, and swung to face Vilenov like a toy on a wire. There was a fluttering roar over Palisades Park. The cliff seemed to tremble. Vilenov looked up and to his left.

Appearing to just clear the rail, a Los Angeles police helicopter loomed enormously. It very slowly turned to face the brush, its rotors creating flurries of leaves. An electronically magnified voice hit the cliff's face like a fist.

"Anyone in the brush is ordered to pull his shirt over his head and crawl on hands and knees to the highway. Once there you are further ordered to lay face down and to not turn your head. If you do so you will be fired upon."

In a minute a couple of transients came slithering onto the highway on their stomachs, shirts over their heads. Half a dozen CHP officers approached in crescent formation, their guns trained on the pair. A man in white shirt and tie stepped through as soon as the two had been pinned by their necks and backs. This officer kicked the derelicts repeatedly, then grabbed a man by the hair and slowly turned his head while holding a massive handgun to the temple. He repeated the process with the second man. After a tense minute he looked up and shook his head emphatically.

The helicopter edged north, still facing the cliff, the cockpit's shotgun officer carefully studying the brush through binoculars. Vilenov drew into a tight, trembling ball. It was like having a tornado sneak up on you. Suddenly wind was lashing his face and hair. The tornado steadied at twelve o'clock.

"You in the brush!"

Vilenov came out of his crouch with all the force of a detonating grenade. As though buffeted by a physical blow, the chopper reared, did a complete back flip, and plummeted spiraling to the crowded highway below. CHP cars began ramming one another, ATVs created erratic patterns in the sand. One drove directly into the surf.

Halfway up the cliff, Vilenov clawed his way to a closed park-to-highway staircase, then bounded up the crumbling cement steps and scrambled over the staircase's locked chain link gate. The park was a bizzaro-world riot. Policemen were clubbing seniors and vagabonds while their huge K9 Shepherds savaged citizens, handlers, and each other. Unnoticed, Vilenov loped back to the bridge, hopped the rail, and tumbled down to the highway. A steaming police cruiser now lay smashed a-gainst a cement retaining wall at the tunnel's entrance, and be-side this car ran a telltale trail of blood drops; zigzagging across the lanes, disappearing down the embankment. Dash, seat, and carpet were flecked and smeared with blood. Finding the key still in the ignition, Vilenov fired her up and made a hard U-turn. He floored the car through the tunnel and onto the 10 free-way. Nobody was going to screw him this time. He flipped off the howling emergency vehicles racing toward the beach.

A lone helicopter rose like a Harpy in his left-hand mir-ror. Vilenov pounded his fist on the steering wheel three times, and the car's windshield cracked, spiderwebbed, and exploded. A flurry of glass chips blew back in his face. He snarled and ac-celerated as a second helicopter, a third, then a fourth, appeared in a long ascending tail.

Eastbound cars, their drivers freaked-out by all the road- and air activity, were creating an irregularly spaced obstacle course. Vilenov cut off and tailgated indiscriminately while trig-gering his lights and siren, causing those already confused drivers to panic. As his rage increased, cars spun out or veered off the freeway. Off-pavement, sporadic events occurred at each new burst of emotion: cracks raced across retaining walls, signs rattled, concussive reports in the scrub were followed by brief wisps of smoke.

Vilenov hurtled across the 405, his anger scattering everything in his path. He threw a quick look back. The chain of helicopters was much nearer, closing in a tight eastbound line; even as he watched, a fifth fell in line high above the fourth. Miles ahead, half a dozen others were circling like gulls riding a lazy current. He pushed the car over 100, thin plumes of smoke rising in the city around him.

And as he accelerated, chips of glass in his hair and the wind in his eyes, he imagined a fleeing figure; stumbling, ex-hausted, regularly looking back, the face taut with terror. Lawrence Abram. Pampered turncoat and thief. And every time that despised face flashed back it was as if a piston had just pounded in Vilenov's skull. He opened and shut his eyes with the piston's rhythm, sensing a seizure coming on. "Not now!"

he whimpered. "Not...*now!*" A succession of small explosions to his left sounded in perfect sync with the piston. On his right a tractor-trailer swerved wildly, the forty-foot trailer disengaging and flipping across the lanes. Vilenov avoided it automatically, going through brake, wheel, and accelerator in one motion. But all he could see was that face!

Sitting straight-up as he drove, he opened his mouth and *just screamed.*

Chapter Eleven

The Impact

Abram tried the downtown number again, and again got the canned voice rerouting him to the other canned voice. And again the other canned voice informed him his call could not be put through. He took a sip and glanced at his watch. Nelson Prentis should have dismissed the press long ago. He should be home by now, or at least be on the short drive down Wilshire. He tried Prentis's cell phone and got nowhere. Abram looked around dully. All the stores on Cadillac and Robertson were closed. Traffic was dead. He dropped in two more quarters and again punched Prentis's home number. And again the DA's voice came in, the familiar recorded message explaining that he was presently unavailable, and wondering if the caller could please leave a message after the tone.

Abram cringed at the beep. "Pick up, Nelson, pick up! It's Larry. I'm at a pay phone. Cadillac and Robertson. I got sick of sitting inside staring at the tube, watching this city go to hell. Nellie...why can't you keep your liquor cabinet stocked? I looked inside and found nothing but ghosts. So I called a cab and went out for a pint, just so's I wouldn't have to be *totally* alone. And when I left the store the cab was history." He closed an eye and appraised the area. "All of a sudden the streets are practically dead. Our boy is on his way, and he's pissed. I can feel it. So just listen, Nelson, I...I brought Pearl with me. I know you told me to never take her down, but this is an *emergency*, and I figured just this *once*." He blew into the phone.

131

"Buddy, I need a ride out. You're probably more aware of what's going on than anybody other than the Chief, but I just got some fresh gumbo over the store owner's CB: Nelson, stampeding idiots have blocked *every* freeway! It's like Godzilla's on the horizon. And I can see the smoke of fires...one, two, three...six of 'em. Now pick up, Nelson, *pick up!*"

The air went dead at the closing tone, but Abram kept right on sputtering into the mouthpiece. "Listen, Nelson, I'm *stuck* here! O*kay*, buddy? But I don't *want* to go back to your place. I need transportation for the family and myself out of the city, and I need it *quick*." He tucked the receiver between his shoulder and jaw, massaging his forehead with one hand while repeatedly clenching the other. His voice rose and fell, lachrymose and begging. "Oh, *buddy*," he whined, "I've already seen some looting, and I just watched a bunch of tourists being stomped *for nothing* over on National! And there wasn't a damned thing a scared-shitless cabbie and lawyer could about it. There's just so much anger and hatred in the air, man. You can feel it. Now I need transportation *out* of here, Nellie! Surely you can get *somebody* to me! *Please!*"

Abram dropped the receiver and let it dangle, pulled the half-consumed pint of rum from under his arm and took another slug. The liquor went down like lava. He opened his briefcase and replaced the bottle. Nestled in a clean folded shirt was Prentis's beloved pearl handled derringer. It was a prized heirloom, kept loaded in a polished walnut saddle on Prentis's mantel, but for show only. He ran his finger along the barrel, covered the gun back up and snapped shut his briefcase.

Lawrence Abram started across Robertson determinedly, obsessed with getting inside a building to privately access his pocket organizer. A lot of people owed him favors.

Halfway across the street he grew aware of whipping lights rounding Beverlywood onto Robertson. Abram almost sagged with relief. His buddy, God bless him, had come through.

Right away he was struck by the ridiculousness of this drunken notion. Abram froze in the police car's headlights, every thought and impulse crunched in a cerebral logjam.

The car hit Abram so hard the attorney was hurled

fifteen yards up Robertson. The driver slammed on the brakes, threw the car in reverse and ran over the body, hammered into drive and ran over it again.

The door flew open and a wild-eyed cop almost fell out, his expression a strange blend of frenzy and horror. He whipped out his handgun and emptied it into the mangled corpse, then continued to work the trigger while his head rocked back and forth. Finally his eyes fell on the briefcase and its scattered contents. He staggered to the derringer, shoved the barrel in his mouth, and desperately pulled the trigger.

Although his recovering mind was urgently focused on the road, Vilenov still managed to keep an eye peeled and an ear pegged. The speeding car was filled with a near-continuous stream of police chatter, and by latching onto familiar street names he was able to glean that not far ahead the 10-110 exchange was in gridlock, and that every available police unit was being dispatched to hold the area against him. As he veered onto the south offramp at National Boulevard the chain of helicopters swung right along behind.

At first glance National appeared deserted. But the moment he rolled off the ramp a single police unit maybe half a mile ahead came to life and raced along with siren blaring and lights burning, clearing the way. The tactic was lost on Vilenov, yet this single glimpse of foreshadowing authority sent him out of his mind with anger. The manifestations of this anger, radiating in all directions, caused rows of shop windows to pop like firecrackers. The incessant radio chatter only ratcheted up his passion. He was just reaching to kill it when a voice sounded so clearly the speaker might have been sitting right beside him in the hurtling car.

"Nicolas Vilenov."

Vilenov took the corner at Venice Boulevard on two wheels, siding smack into the front end of a parked UPS truck. The impact crushed the driver's door and just missed taking off his leg.

"Nicolas Vilenov!"

He gave the car gas, over and over, but the door was solidly impaled on the truck's fender. Only by continuously jerking in forward and reverse was he able to wrench the door from its hinges, and by that time a crowd was all over him. Vilenov cussed them out collectively and shot down Venice. Half a mile ahead, a different black-and-white came to life and sped away, all flashing lights and siren. Vilenov screamed at it, continuing to accelerate while repeatedly kicking his brake foot on the floorboard. To his left a high brick wall collapsed like a house of cards.

"Nicolas Vilenov, this is the Los Angeles Chief of Police speaking. You are ordered to pull over your vehicle, and to surrender at once. All avenues out of the city are blocked; your situation is entirely hopeless. Be advised that troops of the National Guard have been deployed, and will not hesitate to use military weapons."

Vilenov put his fist into the car's padded roof and stomped his feet up and down like a man playing double bass drums. *Go on*, he thought, residential windows blowing out around him, *keep talking. Hog the radio. Don't let anybody else communicate.*

One of the pursuing helicopters, an AH-64 Apache, veered well clear of the chain and emitted a short 30mm burst that disintegrated a billboard just ahead.

Vilenov hit the brakes hard, spun out, and jumped right back on the gas. That was a total bluff—no way would they chance on blowing away civilians. But the spinout threw him south on Centinela; he was now moving away from the beach on a course with few wide-open outlets. The avenue was dead: shops closed, sidewalks clear, streetlamps coming up gold in the setting sun. As he burned through Culver City, Vilenov rediscovered his old cocky self. He drove with his waving left arm thrust out the open driver's side, giving the finger to the patient line of copters. One of rock's great anthems blew through his mind, the lyrics contorting his lips. "I'm getting closer," he sang, "to my home."

Another burst from the Apache's turret demolished a chain link fence dangerously near the clattering cruiser. Vilenov leaned right out of the car as he drove, bawling profanities at the closing copter. The Apache, after bouncing and swaying perilously, veered to the east and hovered at a hundred feet in a southwesterly pitch. In less than a minute it was back on him with an attitude. Vilenov flew across Culver Boulevard while a screaming hail ripped up the road around him. To avoid a very certain and very messy death, he was forced to make a hard right at the dry concrete basin of Ballona Creek.

An inland bike path runs alongside this basin, accessible from north-south roads only by lifting a bike's wheels over a removable locking foot-high steel barrier designed to prevent access to general traffic. Vilenov hit this barrier at almost forty miles an hour, miraculously sparing the tires but warping the front tie rod, crushing the oil pan, and tearing up the transmission. He landed on the rear wheels. Leaving a dozen weaving red and black trails in a miscellany of broken parts, he sped recklessly along the bike path for a hundred yards before taking out the first row of picnic tables.

Half of southern Culver City must have turned out to cheer on Vilenov on this lovely mild summer afternoon. Ballona's bike path was a natural and popular place to congregate, free of cars and commerce. People could hang. Portable televisions and boom boxes were everywhere; folks with binoculars had been excitedly following the line of helicopters while trading observations with friends and families glued to TVs. But, riveted as they were by the cruiser's televised proximity, no one was prepared for the steaming, screeching steel monster that came at them like a bat out of Hell. Chairs and bodies were pummeled by the cruiser's smashed grille, children and portable barbecues flew in through the windshield's frame, battering Vilenov's face and shoulders so that he could only swerve wildly through the thrashing crowd, colliding with some, running over others. He yanked the wheel left and went over the path's lip, twenty feet down the cement grade to the basin's narrow floor, screams of unimaginable horror swirling behind him like a haunted wind.

At this point the Apache dipped its nose and came on hard, firing continuously. Vilenov could only run the car up and down the basin's opposing slopes in a temporary evasive maneuver, the accelerator to the floor. This went on for less than a minute; the cruiser was coming up on Lincoln, where hundreds of spectators were lining the basin and hanging from the overpass. The Apache pulled up sharply as Vilenov hammered up the grade through dozens of scattering bystanders.

He lurched to a stop at Lincoln Boulevard's bike path entrance, barely in time to glimpse a sheriff's car streaking away. The foot-high barrier had just been removed; Vilenov was free to drive straight onto Lincoln. Even as he perched casually with one leg and one arm outside the car, pondering this gambit, he was approached by phalanxes of loud intrepid fools, some calling out threats, some shouting congratulations. Vilenov darkly stepped halfway out of the car, narrowly controlling his passion. One by one the rowdies stepped back. When his path was cleared he sat back down just as meaningfully and slowly motored through the entrance onto Lincoln. He braked instantly—a pair of Army tanks to his left were swinging their cannons his way. Vilenov peeled out to his right and floored the car north, only to find every intersection barricaded by highway patrol cars, by SWAT vans, by a variety of trucks and trailers. He automatically hit the side streets, his wrath popping glass, setting off motion detectors, bringing to full throat every dog in the vicinity. And the farther he drove, the angrier he grew: homeowners, refusing to evacuate their beloved neighborhoods, had erected barriers of cars, RVs, trash cans and mattresses, leaving only confidential routes for their personal ingress and egress. These blocked-off city streets were now silent roads to nowhere. Marina del Rey had effectively become a labyrinth.

But Nicolas Vilenov was back, and he knew this area better than anybody. He shot across vacant lots and down alleys, zigzagged over sidewalks and lawns, swerved to take advantage of every inch of tree cover; always trying to lose the big eye in the sky. By this method he eventually worked his way clear to Washington Boulevard, his lifeline to the beach and Venice Canals. But as he burst clattering and clanging from an alley he was greeted by an unexpected crescent of cars and motorcycles; everything from SMPD to CHP to LAPD. Vilenov didn't even slow. He tore straight into a shocked wedge of motorcycle cops, then, in a bloody rain of flesh and metal, smashed into a cruiser, instantly corrected, and barreled west down Washington. The entire force came after him like savages after a covered wagon. At Lincoln additional knots of official vehicles broke into his wake, quickly joined by motorcycles tearing out of drives and underground garages. The line of helicopters veered, closed, and jumped right on his rocking rear end. He punched on his lights and siren. Vilenov's fuming car became a howling, flashing comet with a growing law enforcement tail.

Then, for no apparent reason, the entire cavalcade backed off, and he found himself screaming toward the beach alone. The mystery was solved when he hit Admiralty Way. An explosion on his car near the grille, and a hundred fragments of his right headlight sparkled, blew outward, and vanished. Before he realized what was happening, police marksmen behind bushes and on corner rooftops were letting go with a volley that tore the cruiser's roof and passenger side to ribbons. Vilenov swerved hard to his left and sped wildly up Admiralty, swiping signs and flowerbeds as he went. The car's hood flew open, slammed against the roof, blew off its hinges in a cloud of steam.

Admiralty was cut off between Sweet Harbor and the Park by sheriff's cars parked bumper to bumper, reinforced with an antique fire truck from the Admiralty station. Crouched behind those cars, and stretched out on their hoods, officers were watching Vilenov come on through their rifles' sights.

At the sound of gunfire he yanked the wheel left, slamming into the curb and blowing the left front tire off its rim. He plowed across the grass onto the bike path, the exposed rim throwing a low plume of sparks all along the asphalt and back onto Admiralty Way. Every car roared to life and tore around the fire truck. Vilenov clung to the rocking wheel, staring straight ahead with his jaws clenched. At least a dozen howling black-and-whites were turning onto Admiralty from Fiji Way, cutting him off completely. His eyes narrowed...were those Humvees pulling up behind them...and now, turning off of Fiji, could those *possibly* be the camouflaged bodies of troop transports? He peered into his side-view mirror. That Apache was no bluff. The goddamned governor had called out the goddamned

Army.

His car slammed and hissed to a halt at the corner of Admiralty and Mindanao. To his left, Lincoln Boulevard's Mindanao access was fully obstructed by used automobiles off Lincoln Ford's adjacent lot. Marina Market's parking was blocked by a broad semi-circle of volunteered private vehicles. Vilenov could either stay put or turn right down the short road to the cul-de-sac of Burton Chace Park. For the first time he was honestly appreciating his enemy. He'd been arrogant enough to pretend he was leading them on a merry chase, rather than being pressed into an evacuated verdant corner. Squinting, he peered down Mindanao and shook his head admiringly.

So this is where they'd orchestrated his demise; a lovely hidden arena, all grass and trees, surrounded by the ever-lapping sea. Very appropriate. Almost considerate. The ranks came to a halt before him, sirens cut. Just behind, the sheriffs' cars were also at rest, idling in line with their roof lights spinning. But soundless. They wanted him to calm down. Now there was nothing to be heard other than the complex thrumming of eight helicopters aligned in a long ascendant tail over Admiralty. As Vilenov watched, a news copter broke rank to swing over Chace.

He yanked the steering wheel to the right. *There'll be hell to pay for that move,* he thought, and gave the car gas. With a groan of tortured springs the cruiser wobbled around the corner and went grinding down the road.

The line of helicopters proceeded along Admiralty until their median copter, the Apache, was hovering directly over the Admiralty-Mindanao intersection and pointing straight at the laboring patrol car. The copter began tailing Vilenov with a progress that was almost imperceptible. In a slow motion aerial ballet, the remaining copters produced a formation like geese on the wing and gradually moved west in the Apache's wake.

Vilenov fought his crippled cruiser to the parking area. He was trying to turn in on the hot rim when a rocket launched from the Apache took out the passenger side and sent the car flying.

The pulse of the situation instantly jumped from tranquil to frantic. In a heartbeat the Apache was hovering right over the

138

mangled car, the air was alive with sirens, and dozens of vehicles were racing down Mindanao.

Vilenov picked himself out of the shrubbery, a mass of cuts and bruises. But very much alive. He was very much alive because he hadn't been wearing a seat belt in a car without a driver's-side door. He'd been flung like a doll in one direction, and the heavy, fiery mass of the cruiser in another. The car had landed on its roof in a tree-lined tiled plaza marking the park's entrance.

He shrank back into the shrubs, blinking rapidly, deliberating...law enforcement's complete attention was focused on the spewing corpse of the upended police car...the Apache was hovering not twenty feet above, its tremendous searchlight fixed on the wreckage...the whole smashed gushing mess was circled by lawmen—in uniforms, in shirts and ties, in jumpsuits and in civvies—their apparel whipping in the rotors' wind. They were approaching with extreme caution, rifles and shotguns extended like men feeling out a cobra's nest. Vilenov took a deep breath and, his nose almost to the ground, ran tiptoeing through the park.

Chace isn't a particularly large park, just ten beautifully landscaped acres tucked between the lazy blue tines of Basins G and H in Marina Channel. There's a community center, a trio of peaked barbecue enclosures, a central courtyard, and a quaint wooden bridge spanning soft green knolls. Vilenov flitted from one bit of cover to the next, a black roving wraith at the far reach of headlight beams. He knew it wouldn't be long before someone in charge sent in the Marines, but he had a plan. While running he studied the sleepy silhouettes of yachts and dinghies, inboards and outboards; all gently rocking side by side in their slips. Only a narrow bike path and short fence separated these boats from the trees and grass. Once he'd pirated a vessel it would be a simple matter of five minutes' silent running and he'd be on the north side of Basin G, slipping away through a new maze of innocent craft. He knew it would take time for his enemies to scour the park; they'd be thorough as hell, and approaching with great care. There were already a number of boats, outsiders attracted or repulsed by all the noise in the air and on the ground, passing back and forth in a quiet, dreamy drift. One more ghost would go unnoticed. He was just stepping over the fence when there came two sharp *blats* of an air horn. The news copter pulled up from low over Basin H and beat in an arc above the park, capturing Vilenov in its searchlight as he straddled the fence. The chopper came on until well over the waters of Basin G. There it hovered, its dazzling light directed at an angle exposing the park's entire tip.

But the moment Vilenov looked up the helicopter was buffeted as though by a great wind. Its tail dipped, and the huge machine dropped like a bomb into the basin. There were shouts in the distance, quickly followed by the bright points of head-lights tearing through the park. Half a minute later Guardsmen were leaping from a transport, their silhouettes flashing through the beams as they ran to line the bridge from both ends. The Apache rose above the trees like a great angry dragonfly, its searchlight's blinding column quickly fixing on the ragged little man dragging his leg back over the fence.

Vilenov turned slowly to face a small army of marks-men, his eyes burning in the white-hot glare. He raised his arms high, but didn't halt in the classic pose of surrender, lowering them gradually to the ten-and two o'clock position while turn-ing the palms inward. Every man facing him recognized the street challenge, and all eyes were instinctively drawn to his. In this way Vilenov visually embraced the whole mass of his en-emy: the dozens of police with handguns poised, the line of National Guardsmen with rifles leveled, the pilot and gunner of the huge green chopper now tilting down its nose with guns and rockets ready. His ugly gray eyes swept side to side and he smiled like a winner, like a man who has done it all. There was a pause; a few excruciating seconds when everyone involved appeared frozen in place.

Nicolas Vilenov made a sudden move as if going for a weapon, and the combined firepower of lawmen, Guardsmen, and attack helicopter blew his vile black soul straight back to Hell.

Chapter Twelve

The End

It was warm as many a summer's day, though most of the pumpkins were history, and Thanksgiving decorations already well on the way up. A few houses were even strung with Christmas lights, and, on the miniature replica lighthouse at Fisherman's Village, a sun-bleached plastic Santa had been crucified to herald the yuletide. Looking past the Village and across the Marina's Main Channel, park goers stood watching the Admiralty Apartments and Marriott Hotel undergoing the final stages of fire damage repair.

And from where Damon leaned on the fence bordering Basin G, it was easy to visualize those fires breaking out, to hear police and emergency vehicles howling in every direction, and to imagine the loose cannon of Nicolas Vilenov breaking all the rules as he barreled along in a stolen, thrashed police car. And whenever Damon turned to critically consider the park, he could picture, equally well, the hot wall of law enforcement storming Vilenov's final stand. Damon had to rely on imagination, for there were no visual records.

But there were a number of *vestiges*, and what amounted to, in Damon's eyes, a virtual shrine. The vestigial evidence consisted of charred branches, half-healed tire grooves, and the occasional wink of a shell casing floating perpetually round the basins. The shrine was a huge space at his left elbow where a chunk had been blown out of the original bike path. This space was now surrounded by a high chain link fence bearing signs warning away children and other scoundrels. Channel water formed a gently slapping pool in the gap.

Damon's reverie was interrupted by a series of increasingly heavy vibrations in the fence. He looked casually to his right and immediately jerked back his head. Shambling along the fence was the most pitiable wino he'd ever seen, dressed in rags over rags, filthier by the layer. The man's trash-tangled, wispy white hair hadn't seen a comb, a bar of soap, or a pair of scissors in years. His face was devastated by a lifetime of alcohol abuse, by physical and emotional suffering, by a million squints and gnashes. Folds of very loose flesh hung like wattles from his chin and jowls. It looked like one more knock on the head would pop his extraordinarily swollen eyes right out of their sockets.

Now, though Damon was a generally compassionate and generous man, he genuinely loathed being approached by the unfortunate. It's just that there were *so* many of these people in the area—and handing out money and advice didn't seem to help a bit. He studied the Marriott resignedly, his train of thought derailed.

The wino snuffled right up next to him and copied his position. Damon stared hard at the water, himself a beggar; every nuance of his body language beseeching the intruder to mooch elsewhere. He thought of faking an emergency bathroom run, or maybe moving along determinedly as though suddenly distracted. He even thought of playing deaf. But the wino didn't move or open his mouth, and time seemed to die. Damon was just turning to walk when the wino hawked one into the water, and so initiated their relationship.

"Helluva job," he sniffed, "patchn up them hotels when they burn. I seen that big one catch, an I thought for sure she'd go all the way."

"They've got super-sophisticated sprinkler systems," Damon alliterated unintentionally, "and the Fire Department is right up the street. Look—"

"Hell!" the wino croaked. "Fire department couldn' get a handle on it! They was spread out thinner'n a church sandwich, an so many cops was chasn that guy they wasn' no fire truck coulda made it down that street. An when he come runnin in the park this place was blocked off solid, man, *solid!* I couldn' show my pretty face or I'da been shot to jesus."

Damon could only recoil (another of his major peeves was hollering strangers). He was just digging for change when the import of the wino's outburst came like a slap across the face.

"You...you actually *saw* Nicolas Vilenov pursued into this park?"

The wino glowered. "What I jus say?"

"What you just said."

"An what I jus said is what I jus said I seen, *okay*? I seen 'em all come in here chasn what's-his-face, an I seen 'em all shoot the whole fuckn place up. Up, down, crosswise, and side-ways."

"Listen, friend," Damon said excitedly. "My name's Raymond Bartholemew Damon, and I write an occasional column for the Argonaut newspaper. You must've seen it."

"Freebie," the wino said contemptuously. "How you make a livn writn for a give-away newspaper?"

"I do other work. I write software and handle some consulting jobs. Look, none of that's important. What *is* important is that I'm researching the whole Vilenov incident for a book I'm writing. There've been a ton of speculative articles and doc-udramas, but as of yet there's nothing to go by other than the official police statement. A civilian's eyewitness account could humanize the whole thing. I'm talking *big* time here. *Millions!"* he ejaculated, and caught himself.

The wino's left eye rolled to study Damon long and dis-dainfully, while his right eye stared across the Marina like a gargoyle's. Finally the left eye swung back to stereo. "I can' talk on a dry belly."

Damon nodded. "Then we'll moisten you right up." He immediately initiated the walk to Marina Market, through the center of the park and down Mindanao, prodding his companion all the way. The wino was surprisingly nimble for a man in his condition, but his tongue was not so swift. He refused to sur-render a morsel of news until he'd encountered that first sweet drop.

143

Damon stopped just outside the market's automated glass doors. "One thing," he said. "Before I invest a single nickel I want to know just where you were when this all came down. I want to know why you were a witness, and I want to know why no one witnessed you being a witness. That park was sealed. After the whole affair the grounds were gone over with a fine-toothed comb."

"But not the water. Coast Guard comes by earlier that day an kicks everbody offa their boats whiles I keeps hunkered low. Wasn a soul but me for miles. After all the 'citement Harbor Patrol comes by an rousts me; tells me I seen nothin, tells me I heared nothin, tells me I wasn never to be seen on the water again. But I comes back anyway. They's a rowboat tied up aside one of the slips, with a blue plastic tarp over her. Me an you was standn almos on top of her in the park, right up by the fence. Tha's my home; tha's my Baby. I been sleepn under that tarp so long," he boasted, "I got keel marks where my ribs useta be. When all the fuss gets goin I wakes up an takes a peeks over the cement an through the fence. I couldn take my eyes offa that whole big trip, man, an I doesn crawl back under Baby's Blanket till it's all over an the cops is pickn up pieces." He licked his lips.

Damon considered the wino's story. "Good enough." He marched right in. A minute later he marched right back out with a pint bottle of Night Train. Against his whispered objections, the wino immediately knocked the bottle back.

Shoppers stopped; some laughing, some frowning. "*Jesus!*" Damon hissed *"Cut it out, will you?"*

The wino ignored him completely. He sucked the bottle dry, staggered back a few paces, turned, and barfed like a dog in one of the little planters between coffee tables.

Damon looked away and nodded. "All right. I think you and I are done exploiting each other here."

The wino whirled, the folds of his face flapping along behind him. He coughed out, desperately, "An I seen more!"

"What more?"

"Everthin! I seen the cops chasn that guy down, an I seen him go nuts, an I seen the cops go nuts right back. But I seen him *walk*, friend. *I seen him walk!*"

The planet screeched to a halt. Damon clenched and un-clenched his fingers. "You...you actually *saw* them gun him down?"

"*No*-o-o-o...I ackchewally *saw* 'em blow away a empty hunka bike path."

"*What?*"

The wino withered at Damon's bark of frustration. He backpedaled urgently. "No, no, friend! No. What I mean is what *you* said."

And it hit Damon: he'd been yanked from the moment the wino'd first opened his gummy manipulating mouth. He grabbed the outermost shirt and shook him so hard the man's head rocked back and forth and side to side. "Now *you're* gonna listen, *friend!* I don't want to hear what you *think* I want to hear, okay? What I want to hear, *straight up*, Dewlap, is what you genuinely *saw*. Is that perfectly clear? You give me the truth and I'll pay you for it, gulp for fact. But if I even *suspect* you're bullshitting me, *man*, we part company." He waited. "Fair?"

"Fair."

"*Fair?*"

"*Fair!*"

Damon dropped his arms. After a long moment he said quietly, "Wait here. Don't you dare move a muscle." He marched right in. Ten minutes later he marched right back out with a full shopping bag.

The wino oozed over. "What you got in the bag? Friend."

"I've got Christmas in the bag. Friend. Enough presents to keep you happy and loquacious."

A quirky pair on a lovely Bay day, the two made their way back to the park by following the walk alongside Basin G's fence, drawing double takes from everyone they passed. The wino appeared none the worse for his experience with the Night Train. "Low—" he tried, "Low...*kway*-shus?"

Embarrassed by all the negative attention, Damon snapped sotto voce, "Means talkative! *Talkative!* Okay?"

"Okay."

"*Okay?*"

"*Okay!*"

"So we're gonna have symbiosis here. *Okay?*"

"Simbe? Sim...simbe?"

"We feed off each other. It's a mutual thing, one-to-one. Look, as long as you keep talking, you keep drinking. You shut up and we split up. Deal?"

"Deal."

"Deal?"

"Deal!"

Damon approached the shrine embracing the bag jealously; the way he saw it, withholding its contents was sweet turnabout for the wino's earlier reticence. Besides, he knew he needed to maintain control of the situation. If his companion got too drunk too fast, it could easily shorten or garble the narrative he was praying for. He instructed the wino to lead him directly to the rowboat. Everything depended on precisely recreating the vantage of that warm summer night. The wino was most uptight about this demand, as it meant breaking his own rule concerning approaching the slips before dark, a full two hours away.

But Damon wasn't farting around. "If you wanna drink, man, then we do this right." He placed the bag to one side of the tall locked gate between the ramp and bike path. He and the wino followed the short fence a ways, then swung their legs over and scooted back along the basin's high cement breakwater, steadying themselves hand over hand while walking on their toes. When they made the gate Damon reached over the fence to retrieve the bag. They tiptoed down the gently rocking ramp and stood amongst the outboards and dinghies. The water showed an oily film. Damon stood watching the marina breathe on the iron lung of progress: garbage drifting in, garbage drifting out. He could see how the bottom half of the wino's rowboat told the uneven tale of this flux. It reminded him of the lower gum line of a chain smoker.

The rowboat, owned by a man who kept a small cabin cruiser moored in the slip, appeared to have been bumping there forever. According to the wino, this owner showed up only rarely, and so far he'd been lucky. Beneath the faded blue tarp was a hull full of trash and various found objects. It smelled like a wino lived in it.

"Phew!" Damon said. "What's the name of your boat,

pal? Old Stinky? Let's air this puppy out."

"*Shhh!*" the wino sprayed, angrily hopping side to side with a finger to his lips, his eyes popping.

Damon stepped into the boat carefully, kicked aside a small mound of trash, and sat with the bag between his knees. The wino parked himself close, like a hungry dog by the table. After a short pause to emphasize his ultimate say in the matter, Damon extracted a quart of Boone's Farm Apple and raised an eyebrow. The wino pounced right on it, swallowing and slobbering horribly, only pausing halfway for a single abbreviated gulp of air. Damon prompted him throughout the ordeal and its aftermath, only to learn that, deals notwithstanding, drinking and conversing were two functions the wino would never be able to handle in conjunction. He realized he'd have to bide his time until the man's basic thirst was sated, so he began studying the park from this wonderfully secure vantage—standing to peer, sitting to think—while the wino violated a large bottle of Cisco Berry. Sightseers, sauntering along the bike path above, appeared more amused than offended by the odd pair, and Damon was eventually able to relax somewhat. Although shadows were growing quite long, he was sure he could see the very spot where the news copter had torn up the basin's rocky bottom. He made mental notes and studied angles, his excitement continuing to grow even as the wino sank deeper into oblivion.

But after half an hour of this he found himself dipping in the bag. Damon casually uncapped a quart of Boone's Farm Strawberry and forced down a third, all the while watching the wooden wino out of the corner of his eye. Finally he kicked the old man's foot to get his attention. The wino snapped out of it and went straight for the bottle.

Damon shook his head. "Uh-uh. You talk first, buddy. I've waited long enough." To underscore his seriousness he put the bottle to his lips and drank heartily.

The wino, barely conscious, behaved like a man who'd been lost for days in the desert. His dry lips cracked open and writhed longingly, his good eye rolled searchingly. The other closed up like it had just been poked. When he realized he'd have to sing for his supper he grudgingly began:

"I was capped for the night an rockn with my Baby,

when I was awoked by this great big ka—*boom!* out by the street. I snuck out my head. They was a whole buncha whirlybirds singn over the park entrance, an a zillion coppers drivn with their sirens an lights an the whole shebang, right up to the fountn. A great big searchlight was over ever blessd one of 'em, an now this other chopper come swingn round above me till I knowed I'da been shot if I evn dares move. But then she pulls over the other side an keeps low on the water. She kicks off her light an kinda mellows. Pretty soon I sees this guy come runnin toward me through the park, movn tree to tree. He's all cut up an flittn like a ghost, his tore up ol shirt flappn behind him." The wino caught his breath and turned to stone, eye rolled back and mouth agape.

Damon took a long drink and nodded; first with slow analysis, then with hard certainty. He swished what was left in the bottle and the wino's eye came alive. Damon handed it over, then fished in the bag while the old man went to town. He pulled out a bottle of Merlot, knocked in the cork with the shaft of a screwdriver that had been rolling against his foot, and took a careful swallow. Damon, only an occasional drinker, had a good buzz on. He couldn't imagine what kept the wino going. After a minute he nudged the man's knee with the bottle. The wino dropped his empty amidst a hundred others and began hyperventilating. Damon nudged him again, harder this time. The wino blurted out, "So the guy come runnin up to the fence!" and zoned out completely.

Damon kicked him a good one. The wino's butt bounced off the board as if he was spring-loaded. He pointed theatrically at the sealed-off gap in the bike path beside the water. "An he steps half-over like he's plannin on maybe moseyin down this ramp, same as we done. But then that one chopper makes a couple honks an comes up over the park. The guy steps back onto the path an stares at it while it moves over the water. It puts a big light on him. Suddenly the guy jus *snaps!* He looks up, man. He looks up at that great big holymama bird right where she's floatn, man, right...right...*there!*" The wino pointed to a spot above the water maybe forty feet from Baby. "He looks up like he wants to kill it, an the damn thing goes tail-down *smash* into the water. The waves offa that thing almos capsizes Baby, an while I'm hangn on I hears *another!* chopper, an pokes my head back up. The whole goddam knighted states army come runnin and drivn through the park. They all fans out in a big long line on the bridge an points everthin what they got at him. An he jus smiles."

Damon's jaw dropped. The wino's description was eerily similar to the scene as he'd imagined it a hundred times: the cocky desperado; spitting blood and bile, cornered but not cowed. Then the callous, the inhumane—nay, the *inhuman* overkill of law and order. Damon's mind fast-forwarded to an enticingly-near future, when a jaded world responds to a searing manuscript bursting through the rumors and emotional haze. R.B. Damon, the reporter who walked the extra mile, the unsung genius who made the hard truth painfully clear to anyone with a shred of conscience...the man who, uncomfortable with all the lights and groupies and hoopla, stood like a rock before his gaping contemporaries and humbly accepted the Pulitzer. But not for himself, goddamn it. For The People!

And now the sun's perfect rim was clipped by the horizon. "Go on," Damon's voice rumbled from his dream. "You were spraying?"

The wino took a deep breath. "An he jus stans there, with his arms all spread out like that Sherman on the mountain guy, as if he's embracn 'em all, an he looks ever one of 'em in the eye while the news chopper goes down kickn."

Damon nodded, sighed, and swallowed manfully. He shook his head with wry gravity. "And then they blew his poor ass away with everything they had."

"No...*no!*...an *then* he walks along the rail jus as calm as calm can be, an hops over the fence by Baby here. An he clims aboard the *Harbor Belle* like he owns her, fires her up an heads on out the channel. He didn see me. We was both starin at the park. Suddenly the whole freakn Army come down on that bike path all at once. I seen 'em shoot tommy guns an 'zookers, an shotguns and rifles an hanguns too. An I seen that great big green chopper unload three rockets on that spot. When the fireworks was all over they was nothn but a giant chunk the size of a house blastd outta that path, an so much smoke in the air I hadda crawl back under Baby's Blanket to breathe."

Damon sucked down the Merlot thoughtfully, mentally revisiting all those rumors of his man altering the perception of onlookers. Very gradually, very tentatively, that old private smile enveloped the bottle's heavy glass mouth...ludicrous or not, the whole concept was delicious—to be able, as a male, to do what you want, to take what you want, and not have to answer to all the silly artificial crap of society. To not have to be *domesticated*. No tepidity. No compromise...over the last couple months a huge confused cult had grown around Vilenov's supposed supernatural abilities, and made his memory appealing to every healthy male ego sick of having basic urges demonized or commercialized. Much of Vilenov's appeal lay, perversely, in the fact that his memory *could not* be commercialized. No major franchise wanted to gamble on glamourizing a rapist. But, as the archetypal Bad Boy, he'd rapidly become irresistible as a rebel figure. Even nice-guy Damon, although outwardly focused on his project, was privately enthused by the fantasy of an instantly pliable femininity, suddenly docile bullies, and throngs of useless loitering idiots reacting positively to his creative ideas. It's all about *power*...but power has to be used wisely. That's the kicker. How in God's name can a man bring all these flaunting bimbos to their knees, force the fatcats and weasels to surrender their ill-gotten gains, pull all the fly-covered, mud-caked, Koran-thumping Third world bastards into the 21st century, damn it, without being the heavy? Real power is a primitive quality, requiring its holder to wield without conscience, without compassion. Damon, like all decent men, just wanted things right in the world. He knew he'd never have the cool to stomp here, to stand there. And *that* was Vilenov's true appeal. He didn't have a conscience. He was a freak, a throwback, a dauntless representative of a time when men were men, instead of a bunch of spiritually-challenged weenies under the whip of Woman and Law. Wannabe-men like Damon lived vicariously through the legend's exploits, and so survived to grovel another day.

Now he was alternately nodding and shaking his head, wanting to believe. And when he spoke his voice seemed detached, as though it belonged to some future campfire storyteller: "You know...they never *did* recover a body. They fig-

ured he'd been turned into fried fish food—blasted into fragments and gone with the tide."

Another voice snapped him out of it. "Oh, he's gone
with the tide, all right. Oughta be comn up on T'iti bout now."

Damon began chugging wine in his excitement. He'd
become quite drunk, but the gleam in his eyes belied his condition. He passed the Merlot, found a pen in his shirt pocket,
tore a large piece off the brown paper bag. "The *Harbor Belle*,
you say? Outboard or inboard? How many feet would you
estimate?"

The wino huffed while his left eye burned. A dark stain
formed in the crotch of his pants. "What do I know bout all that
stuff…it was a little job, *dammit*, a motorboat!"

Damon tore the bottle from his hands. "*I need details!*"

But the wino snatched the neck right back, put the bottle
to his lips and drank furiously, his flickering eye glued to the reporter. Damon shrugged angrily and reached between his knees
for the crown jewel. He unscrewed the cognac's cap and lovingly raised the bottle to his lips, took a long, exaggerated swallow.
The wino's face fell. The reporter gently bounced the bottle a-
gainst his knee, letting the wino know its dispensation was iffy.
"*So*, you blurry son of a bitch, you fantasized the whole fucking
thing, didn't you?"

"I didn fansize nuthn, man. *Nuthn!* If I said I seen what I
said I seen, then I seen what I said I said I seen…*man!*"

Damon angrily handed over the cognac. "Oh…just *mellow out*, man! Don't go getting your gonads all in a knot! And
don't swallow so fast. You'll just end up puking again…*man*."

The wino tore the bottle from Damon's hand and drank
more than any man should be able. He held the bottle to his
chest warningly, blood and brandy flowing from his nostrils.

"No puke! No nuthn! I seen him step back over the rail
an shimmy down here while the cops an the copters an the tanks
an the submarines shot fire an bullits an everthin what they had
on that one fuckn pisspoor spot, *man!* They shot it up, they blew
it up, they sent zappers an boms an all hellfire outta the sky *on
that one spot, man*, right after that forin guy clims over the rail
almos nex to me, gets on the *Belle* an sails off…off…" He
pointed at the channel. "Outta here! Gone! An nobody seen it

but me!" His head dropped between his knees, the cognac bottle falling upright in the trash. "No bullshit," he whimpered. A string of saliva rolled off his lower lip and dangled till it kissed the rowboat's filthy keel. *"Nuthn!"*

He remained in that hunched position, barely alive; a sick ugly statue rocking with the Marina. Damon was studying him blearily when a gorgeous yacht cruised past, its wake rocking Baby harder. His mouth fell open and he almost wept with want. But his pain was short-lived. Soon, Damon knew, a similar vessel would be his.

Because he'd made up his mind on the spot. Raymond Damon was no biographer. He was going after Nicolas Vilenov in the flesh, and he would pursue him across the seven seas. A piece of his personality challenged him to name all seven seas, but another piece was flustered by the direct definition of a *sea* as opposed to an *ocean*. He tried anyway, counting oceans on a hand. When he ran out of fingers his eye fell on the half-full bottle of cognac, rocking precariously between the wino's tatterdemalion shoes. In a breathtaking move, he snatched the bottle by its neck before the rowboat's motion could claim it. Damon smirked. He'd always known he could have played for the big leagues. He took a swallow, squeezed shut his eyes, and began rocking in syncopation with Baby. When he reopened his eyes it was dusk. He turned his head and mumbled to the wino, "So *tell* me, my oh-so wise and worldly friend. Tell me…is this steamer *really* yours?"

The wino snapped up like he'd been kicked. *"Mine!* My boat, goddam you, *mine!* Sloop John me…sloojohn…sloop…"

"Avast!" Damon giggled. "Avay! So *you*, my good man… *you're* the skipper of this gallant seagoing vessel?"

"Mine, gawwwwwd…*dam* you! Ankers way! Yoyos an Ho-Hos an a bottle of…*Mad Dog*. Tha's *me*, matey! So, le's go, le's go. Toe-ko to Soho, way we go."

Damon darkened. He shuddered hard, twice, and his esophagus relaxed. "*I*, my good man," he managed, "am naming *you* my mate. Henceforth you will address me only as 'Captain.' Are we clear here?"

"Aye aye, Cap'n! Ankers way!"

Now Damon, in his logy skull, strutted around an imaginary deck. "And *we*, my loyal sailor and friend, are off on the adventure of a lifetime. We're going to pursue Mr. Vilenov and bring him to justice. And when we're both rich and famous we're gonna buy us an island somewhere and live happily forever and ever after. Are you with me, sailor?"

"Aye aye...I...Aye...I can' sail on a dry belly."

"Then we'll moisten you right up." Damon swallowed liberally and passed the bottle. Suddenly his liver was thumping in his gut. He embraced his waist and bent over till his nose was grazing the keel.

The wino killed the bottle and dropped it amidst the rest. "Okay, Cap'n! Ready to sail!"

Damon collapsed in the fetal position, clutching his stomach. "Okay, matey," he whispered. "But me timbers is... shiverin'. Just let me catch me breath here...first...and we'll be off."

"Aye aye, Cap'n!"

The wino loomed there, watching and waiting, until he was claimed by booze and gravity. His head dropped a few inches at a time, finally lighting on Damon's heaving chest. He stuck his hands between his thighs, curled up his knees, and let the black wave of sleep take him down.